W9-AHN-713

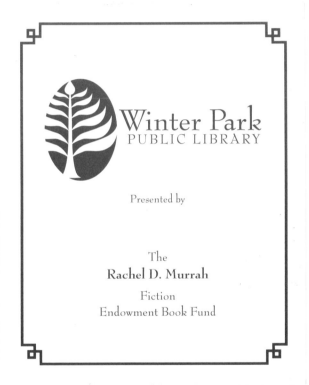

Winter Park
PUBLIC LIBRARY

Presented by

The
Rachel D. Murrah
Fiction
Endowment Book Fund

Reflections *of* Yesterday

Center Point
Large Print

Also by Debbie Macomber and available from Center Point Large Print:

A Turn in the Road
A Girl Like Janet
Undercover Dreamer
Heartsong

**This Large Print Book carries the
Seal of Approval of N.A.V.H.**

Reflections *of* Yesterday

DEBBIE MACOMBER

CENTER POINT LARGE PRINT
THORNDIKE, MAINE

This Center Point Large Print edition is published
in the year 2014 by arrangement with
Harlequin Books S.A.

Copyright © 1986 by Debbie Macomber.

All rights reserved.

All characters in this book have no existence outside the
imagination of the author and have no relation whatsoever
to anyone bearing the same name or names. They are not
even distantly inspired by any individual known or
unkown to the author, and all incidents are pure invention.

The text of this Large Print edition is unabridged.
In other aspects, this book may vary
from the original edition.
Printed in the United States of America
on permanent paper.
Set in 16-point Times New Roman type.

ISBN: 978-1-62899-058-4

Library of Congress Cataloging-in-Publication Data

Macomber, Debbie.
Reflections of yesterday / Debbie Macomber. —
    Center Point Large Print edition.
pages ; cm
ISBN 978-1-62899-058-4 (library binding : alk. paper)
1. Large type books. I. Title.
PS3563.A2364R46 2014
813'.54—dc23

                                            2014002527

To High School Sweethearts Everywhere

Reflections of Yesterday

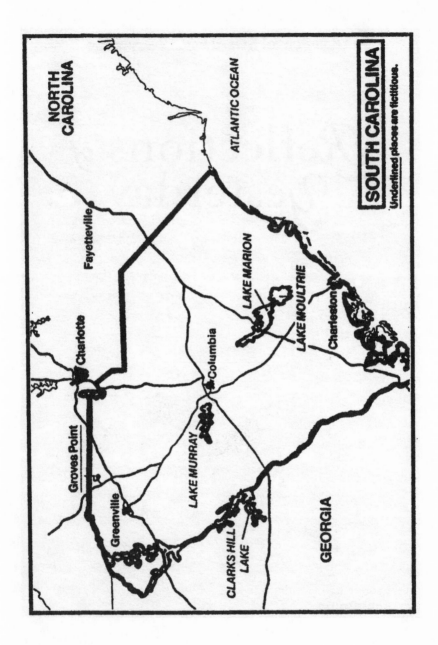

SOUTH CAROLINA

Underlined places are fictitious.

 Prologue

An iridescent moon lit up the ebony sky above Groves Point, South Carolina. Simon Canfield sat in his Mercedes, opening one aluminum can after another until he'd downed the six-pack. Beer cooled the burning ache in the pit of his stomach. Beer helped him remember. For three hundred and sixty-four days of the year he successfully curtailed thoughts of Angie. Only on June 7 did he pull out the memories, roll them around in his tortured mind and relive again the golden days of his abandoned youth.

After ten years it astonished him that the memory of her passionate young body under his held such power. Closing his eyes produced a flood of images, and a sensation of almost painful pleasure. He hated her, and in the same breath realized that he'd go to his grave never having loved another woman the way he'd loved Angie. Only thoughts of her were capable of reducing him to this pensive melancholy. Rarely did he indulge himself the way he had tonight.

Normally, Simon Canfield lived his life as a respected citizen, vice-president of the local bank, the man who made decisions that set the course of an entire community.

Tonight he drank beer instead of whiskey sours.

Tonight he wore jeans instead of a pin-striped suit. Tonight he yearned for a time long past, and the young man who had loved with a passion he never hoped to recapture.

Simon's grip compressed around the hard steering wheel. The pleasure of those youthful days had been swept away by the pain that had followed in the backwash of her deception.

A turn of the key fired the car engine to life. Simon drove carefully, his sleek 450 SL cruising through the dark streets unnoticed. His first stop was outside the Catholic church, St. Elizabeth's. His figure hadn't darkened the doorway in ten years. Fleetingly he wondered if the priests kept the church doors locked these days.

Without conscious direction he headed through town, ignoring the changing message of the time and temperature flashing from the sign above the bank. In the still, silent streets he drove over the railroad tracks until he was parked outside of Angie's old house. The white paint had peeled and the flower beds were sadly neglected, the once well-groomed lawn forsaken. A string of toys and a tricycle on the sidewalk assured him the house wasn't empty. Somehow, Simon doubted that the halls rang with music as they once had.

A surge of anger rose within him until the taste of bitterness erupted in his mouth. He'd wanted children even then. They'd talked about what they would do if Angie were to have a baby. Ironically, their last conversation had been over the possibility of her being pregnant. He could picture her as clearly today as he had ten years before; her long brown hair had been pulled away from her face and tied back with a red chiffon scarf, her brown eyes as round as a deer's, mirroring her troubled soul. She'd looked so unhappy, but had quietly assured him that there wasn't any need to worry, she wasn't pregnant. Dear Lord, he wished she had been.

Now there would be no children for him. He was twenty-seven, and with one disastrous marriage in his wake, he wasn't about to try again. He'd like to blame Angie for that fiasco. But he was the one who'd been fool enough to marry a woman he didn't love, and he had paid dearly for the mistake. He wouldn't marry again.

The ache grew within him until his chest hurt with the intensity of it. Dear Lord, he'd loved Angie.

Simon drove around for what seemed like hours, not surprised that his unplanned route led to the backwoods. His parents had owned these twenty acres. Simon had purchased the land after his divorce from Carol was final. He'd built the house a year later. But it wasn't the welcoming of his home he sought now. Instead, Simon drove down the long driveway that stretched from the road to the back of his house. The harsh slam of his car door echoed through the quiet night. Enough was enough. The ax was stored in the garage and with an impatience he couldn't understand, Simon fetched it, then carried it deep into the twenty acres to the small clearing. He hadn't come here in years, and the memories this land evoked were bittersweet. But Simon had neither the patience nor the desire to explore its significance.

He located the large pecan tree with some difficulty. The only light was the silken rays of a distant moon, slowly creeping toward the horizon.

On the first swing, the ax met the tree's bark with an unrestrained violence. The second and third that followed were born of anger and frustration. Blow followed blow, and he paused only once, to remove his shirt. Uncaring, he tossed it aside and resumed his task until his muscles quivered with the effort and his shoulders heaved with exertion.

The huge tree began to fall, and a panting Simon stood back. His lungs hurt as he sucked in huge gulps of air. His naked torso glistened with perspiration in the glow of the moonlight.

"It's over," he mumbled, chest heaving, as the mighty pecan slammed against the earth.

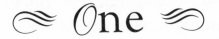

One

The day was flawless as only Groves Point could be in the summer. The golden sun shone brightly from a sky as clear as the Caribbean Sea. Angie Robinson stood outside the hotel. Her fingers toyed nervously with the room key in her pocket as she glanced down Main Street.

Nothing was different, but everything had changed. A traffic signal had been added in front of Garland Pharmacy, and the JCPenney store had installed a colorful awning to shade the display windows. The beauty shop was in the same location, but the neon sign flashed a new name—Cindy's.

Drawing in a deep breath to calm herself, Angie walked toward the bakery at the end of the block. A quick survey inside revealed that the small Formica tables and the ever-full, help-yourself coffeepot were still there. But Angie didn't recognize the middle-aged woman behind the counter. The clerk caught her eye through the large front window and smiled. Angie's smile in return felt stiff and unnatural.

She crossed the street and was halfway down the second block before she noticed that the bank had put up a sign that alternately flashed the temperature and the time of day. For a full minute she stood in a daze, watching as if it could tell her what would happen once she walked inside the double glass doors.

Angie had expected to feel a surging wave of bitterness and anger, but none came. Only a blank, desolate feeling. A hollow emptiness that was incapable of echoing in the dark emotion that had dictated her life these past twelve years.

She took a step in retreat, swiveled and walked away. Not yet, she thought. She'd been in town only a few minutes. A confrontation so soon would be unwise.

Crossing the street at the light, Angie's quick-paced steps led her to the beauty salon. Cindy would tell her everything she needed to know. Cindy had been her friend. Her best friend.

"Can I help you?" A blue-eyed blonde at the reception desk glanced curiously at Angie. The girl transferred a wad of gum from one side of her mouth to the other as she waited for Angie's response.

"Is Cindy available?" she asked, trying to keep her voice even.

"Sure, she's in the back room. If you'll wait a minute, I'll get her."

"Thank you."

The girl slid off the stool and headed for the back of the salon. Empty chairs and a stack of magazines invited Angie to sit down, but for now she preferred to stand.

The bead curtain that covered a rear doorway made a jingling sound as a tall brunette appeared. Two steps into the room she paused in mid-stride. "Oh, my heavens, Angie." A rumbling laugh followed. "Oh, heavens, girl, where have you been all these years?" Before another moment passed, Angie was hauled into open arms and hugged as if she were a lost child returned to a worried mother. "Oh, Lord, I don't believe it." A hand gripping each shoulder pushed Angie back. "Let me look at you. You haven't changed at all."

A smile lit up Angie's soft, brown eyes. Cindy was one person she could always count on welcoming her. "Neither have you."

The musical sound of Cindy's laughter followed. "When did you get in town?"

"Just a few minutes ago." Angie felt breathless and a little giddy. Her friend looked wonderful. Cindy had been the tallest and thinnest girl in class; now she possessed the womanly curves that rounded out her height.

"Can you stay?"

"I'm only here for a couple of days."

"Dear heaven," Cindy murmured and released a long, slow sigh, "it's good to see you."

Her friend's unabashed enthusiasm for life had always been infectious. Angie had often thought that if someone could tap into Cindy's knack for seeing the bright side to everything, the world would be a much happier place. "Tell me about everyone. I'm dying to know what's been going on in Groves Point."

"Filling you in on the last . . . twelve years . . . has it really been that long?" Cindy shook her head in slow amazement. "Mimi, I'll be at the King Cole's. Call me if something disastrous comes up."

Mimi smiled. "Don't worry, I'll hold down the fort."

King Cole's was one of three restaurants in town. The food had always been moderately good and relatively cheap. Angie's father used to take her there for dinner once a month on payday. She'd never told him that she would have preferred hamburgers at the A & W on the outskirts of town.

"Bernice," Cindy cried out as they slid into the upholstered vinyl booth. "Bring us a pair of javas."

"You got it." The slim waitress in the pink uniform brought out two cups of coffee.

"You remember Bernie, don't you?" Cindy prompted. "She was a couple of classes behind us."

For the life of her, Angie didn't, but she pretended to, smiling up at the waitress who looked as blank as Angie. "Good to see you again, Bernice."

"You too." She set the beige mugs on the

Formica tabletop. "You want cream with this?"

"No, thanks."

With a slow gait, Bernice returned behind the counter.

"We tried to get hold of you for the ten-year reunion," Cindy said with a hint of frustration. "But no one knew where you were."

"Charleston."

"Really? Bob and I were there just this summer."

"You married Bob." That deduction wasn't one of her most brilliant, she thought. Cindy and Bob had dated exclusively their senior year.

"Going on eleven years now. We've got two boys. B.J.'s ten and Matt's eight."

"Wonderful." Angie couldn't have meant that more. Her childhood friend deserved a life filled with happiness.

"Bob was in the service for a time and I went to beauty school in Fayetteville and lived with my aunt." Her finger made lazy circles around the rim of the mug as she spoke. "What about you? The last thing I remember is that you were working as a clerk at the pharmacy."

Angie stared into the dark depths of the coffee cup. "Dad and I moved the February after graduation." Neither mentioned that she had left Groves Point without a word or a forwarding address. Not in twelve years had she contacted anyone.

"Remember Shirley Radcliff?"

Angie wasn't likely to forget her. Simon's mother had been furious when he'd asked Angie to the Senior Prom instead of Shirley.

"What ever became of Shirley?" The muscles of her stomach knotted. If Mrs. Canfield had gotten her way Shirley would have married Simon.

"She married a guy in real estate. From what I understand, they're living high off the hog in Savannah. No kids, mind you. It would ruin their life-style."

A smile tugged at the corner of Angie's mouth. No, Shirley wouldn't be the type to appreciate children.

"Gary Carlson's a lawyer in Charlotte. He's married and has a daughter. And Sharon Gleanson's a stewardess."

"I don't believe it." Angie couldn't control a soft laugh. Sharon had always been overweight and extremely shy.

"What about you Angie? Are you married? Do you have children?"

For an instant, one crazy instant, she hesitated. "No to both." Averting her gaze, fearing what her eyes would reveal, Angie asked, "What about Simon? Whatever happened to him?"

"You two were really thick for a while, weren't you?" She didn't wait for Angie to reply. "He married a girl from college, I can't recall her name offhand . . . Carol, I think. It didn't last long, two, three years. Simon's kept to himself since."

"Is he at the bank?" The question was unnecessary, Angie already knew without having to ask, but she had to do something to disguise the pain that seared her soul. So he had married. She'd known it, in her heart she'd always known it. Angie had assumed that after all these years what Simon did couldn't hurt her anymore. But she was wrong. Dead wrong.

"His daddy's the president and Simon's the vice-president. But these days I think Simon runs most everything. He's gotten to be a real stuffed shirt, if you know what I mean."

Angie did. Simon had become the mirror image of his father in spite of his best intentions.

Cindy downed the last of her coffee. "Listen, I've got to get back to the shop. Mrs. Harris, my two o'clock appointment, just arrived. Can you come to dinner tonight? I'll see if I can get a few of the ol' gang together."

"That'd be great. But don't go to any trouble."

"Are you kidding, I haven't got time. Come around six-thirty. We're in the old Silverman place across the street from the park."

"Sure, I remember it. I'll see you tonight."

Cindy pulled some change from her pocket. "Coffee's on me."

"Thanks."

Angie left King Cole's with a sense of exhilaration. After everything that had happened in the past twelve years, she had thought she'd hate Groves Point. But it wasn't in her. The best times of her life had happened in this small community. As much as she'd wanted to blot out the past, it was impossible. Glenn had tried to explain that to her, but she hadn't understood. Now she did. He had been right to tell her she had to confront the past before looking to the future. She'd known that, too, but the past was so painful that it had seemed simpler to ignore the hurt and go on with her life.

The urge to talk to Glenn directed her back to the hotel. Her room was clean, but generic. A double bed, nightstand, dresser and chairs made up the room's furnishings. The one window looked over Main Street, and from where she stood, Angie could see the sign above the bank. An indescribable pain flashed through her. Angie reached for the phone.

"Glenn Lambert."

The warm familiarity of his voice chased the chill from her blood. "Angie Robinson here."

"Angie," he said softly. "How was the trip?"

"Uneventful."

"And Groves Point?"

She smiled gently. "The same. I looked up an old friend who clued me in on what's been happening. The class brain's a lawyer and the shyest girl at Groves Point High is a stewardess."

"I thought you were the class brain," he said with a chuckle.

"Gary and I shared the honors."

A short silence followed. "I miss you, Babe."

Angie always felt uncomfortable when he called her that, but she'd never told Glenn. "I miss you too."

"I wish I could believe that." A trace of impatience tinged his voice, but he disguised it behind a cheerful invitation. "When you come home I'm going to cook you the thickest steak in Charleston."

"I'll look forward to that."

"Good. Have you finished . . . your business yet?"

Glenn didn't know exactly what it was she had to do in Groves Point, and Angie had never explained. That lack of trust had hurt Glenn, and she felt a twinge of guilt. Glenn was the best thing to happen in her life in twelve years. "I've only been in town an hour." But it had to be today. The banks were closed on weekends.

"Will you call me tomorrow?"

"If you want."

"I want you for the rest of my life, Angie. I love you."

"I love you, too," she echoed softly. "I'll talk to you tomorrow." Gently, she replaced the receiver in its cradle.

Talking to Glenn reinforced her determination to be done with the purpose of her visit. A quick check in the mirror assured her that she was now a composed, mature woman. Simon Canfield, Sr. would be incapable of destroying her as he had so long ago.

Not once on the walk to the bank did Angie hesitate. Her heart leaped to her throat as she pushed the glass door that opened into the interior. That, too, hadn't changed. Marble pillars, marble floors, marble hearts.

The teller gave no indication that she recognized her, but Angie remembered Mrs. Wilson, who had been with Groves Point Citizens Federal for years.

"I'd like to see Mr. Canfield," she announced in a crisp voice.

Mrs. Wilson's lined face revealed nothing. "Do you have an appointment?"

"No, but I'm confident he'll see me." She wasn't the least bit sure, but Mrs. Wilson didn't know that. "Tell him Angie Robinson is here."

Again Mrs. Wilson's features remained stoic. "If you'll wait a moment." She left Angie standing on the other side of the counter as she walked the length of the bank and tapped against a frosted glass door. She returned a minute later, her face a bright red hue. "Mr. Canfield suggests . . ." she started, then swallowed with difficulty. "He would prefer not to see you, Ms. Robinson."

How dare he! Angie fumed inwardly, but gave a gracious smile to the teller. "Thank you for your trouble."

The older woman gave her a sympathetic look. "Nice seeing you again, Angie."

"Thank you."

Her heels made sharp, clicking sounds against the marble floor as she turned and walked toward the exit. How dare he humiliate her like this! He had no right. None. With one hand against the metal bar on the glass door, Angie forcefully expelled her breath. She wasn't scum he could walk over. She wouldn't let him.

With an energy born of anger and pride, she pivoted sharply and walked the length of the bank lobby, her chin tilted at a proud angle. She wasn't a member of the country club, nor had she been a member of the upper-class, but she was going to have her say to Simon Canfield, Sr. whether he wanted to hear her or not.

Not bothering to knock, Angie let herself in to the office. "Excuse me for interrupting . . ." She stopped and swallowed back the shock. It wasn't Simon's father who rose from the large oak desk to confront her, but Simon. Time had altered his dark good looks. The gray eyes that had once warmed her with his love were now as cold and grim as the storm-tossed North Sea. Tiny lines fanned from them, but Angie was convinced he hadn't gotten them from smiling. He was so cold that in his gray flannel suit he resembled a stone castle whose defenses were impenetrable. Cold and cruel. The edge of his hard mouth twisted upward. "Hello, Angie."

"Simon." The oxygen returned to her lungs in a deep breath.

Neither spoke again. The chill in the room was palpable, Angie mused, and a smile briefly touched her eyes. It hadn't always been that way with them. Years ago, the temperature had been searingly high, and they couldn't stay out of each other's arms.

"Something amuses you?"

"No." If anything, the thought should produce tears. But Angie hadn't cried in years. Simon had taught her that. She lowered her gaze to the desk top. Crisp, neat, orderly.

"You wanted to see me?" he began in starched tones.

"I wanted to see your father."

"He isn't well. I've assumed most of his duties."

They were speaking like polite strangers. . . . No, Angie amended the thought. They were facing each other like bitter adversaries.

"I'm sorry to hear about your father."

"Are you?" He cocked a mocking brow.

"Yes, of course." She felt flustered and uneasy.

24

"I'd have thought you hated him. But then, it must be difficult to dislike someone who has been so generous with you in the past."

Simon's biting comment was a vivid reminder of the reason for her being in Groves Point. The color flowed from her face, leaving her sickly pale. "Taking that money has always bothered me," Angie confessed in a weak voice that she barely recognized as her own.

The pencil Simon was holding snapped in two. "I'll just bet it did. Ten thousand dollars, Angie? I'm surprised you didn't want more."

"Want more?" she repeated, her heart constricting painfully. "No." Slowly, she shook her head from side to side. She wouldn't bother to explain that it'd nearly killed her to accept that.

Her fingers fumbled at the snap of her purse and were visibly shaking as she withdrew the narrow, white envelope. "I'm returning every penny, plus ten percent compounded interest. Tell your father that I . . ." She hesitated. "No. Don't tell him anything."

"I don't want your money." Simon glared accusingly at the envelope on the edge of his desk.

"It was never mine," Angie said, her voice laced with sadness. "I took it for Clay."

"My, my, aren't you the noble, self-sacrificing daughter?"

The words hurt more than if he'd reached out

25

and slapped her. Involuntarily, Angie blanched. "It bought you your freedom," she managed awkwardly. "I would have thought you'd treasure your marriage more. You paid enough for it."

It looked for a moment as if Simon wanted to physically lash out at her. His fists knotted at his sides, the knuckles whitening.

"I didn't mean that," she whispered, despising their need to hurt each other. "I know you won't believe this, but I wish you well, Simon."

He didn't answer her, instead his troubled gaze narrowed on the envelope.

"If you don't want the money," she murmured, her gaze following his, "then give it to charity."

"Maybe I will," he said and his lip curved up in cynical amusement. "I believe that was my father's original intent."

To her dismay, Angie sucked in a hurt gasp. Slowly the ache in her breast eased so that she could speak. "Oh, Simon, you've changed. What's made you so bitter?"

His short laugh was mirthless. "Not what, but who. Leave, Angie, before I do something we'll both regret."

With an inborn dignity and grace, Angie turned and placed her hand on the doorknob. But something deep within her wouldn't allow her to walk out the door.

"Go ahead," he shouted.

"I can't," she murmured, turning back. "It's

taken me twelve years to come back to this town. Twelve years, Simon." Her voice was raised and wobbled as she fought to control the emotion. "I refuse to have you talk to me as though I did some horrible deed. If anyone should apologize it's you and your family."

"Me?" Simon nearly choked. "You're the one who sold out, so don't play Joan of Arc now and try to place the blame on someone else."

"I did it for you," she cried.

His harsh laugh was filled with contempt. "Only a moment ago you did it for Clay, or so you said."

Angie swallowed back the painful lump that tightened within her throat. Sadly she shook her head. "I'm sorry, Simon, sorry for what happened and sorry for what you've become. But I won't accept—"

"Our love had a price tag—ten thousand dollars," he shouted. "It was *you* who took that money and left. So don't try to ease your conscience now." Leaning forward, he rested the palms of his hands on the edge of the desk. "Now I suggest that you leave."

"Goodbye, Simon."

He didn't answer but turned and faced the window that looked out onto the parking lot.

The door made a clicking sound as she let herself out. Several pairs of eyes followed her progress across the marble floor. Undoubtedly her sharp exchange with Simon had been heard by half the people in the bank. A rush of color invaded her pale face, but she managed to keep her unflinching gaze directed straight ahead as she returned to the hotel.

The key to the hotel room wouldn't fit into the lock as Angie struggled to keep her hand steady. She felt as if her legs were made of rubber. By the time she'd manipulated the lock, she was trembling and weak.

A soft sob erupted from her throat as she set her purse on the dresser. The sound of her cry pierced the silence in the room. Angie's hand gripped the back of the chair as another cry followed the first. Tears blurred her eyes so that the view from the third-story window swam in and out of her vision.

At first she struggled to hold back the emotion, disliking the weakness of tears. Her fingers wiped the moisture from her cheek as she began to pace the room, staring at the ceiling. Another moan wouldn't be denied, and soon every breath became a heart-wrenching cry for all the pain of a love long past. Despair overtook her as she fell across the bed and buried her face in the pillow, crying out a lifetime of agony. She cried for the mother she had never known. And the weak father whom she loved. She cried for the empty promises of her father's dreams, and the Canfield money that had given him the chance to fulfill them. And she cried for a town divided by railroad tracks that made one half unacceptable to the other and had doomed a love from the start.

Biting into her lower lip to forestall the soul-racking sobs, Angie attempted to concentrate on Glenn. Fresh tears filled her eyes. Glenn loved her enough to force her to settle the past. He loved her enough to want her for his wife.

Twisting around, Angie stared out the window at the blue sky. She wept for Glenn, the man she wasn't sure she could marry.

And for Simon, the man she had.

∼ TWO ∼

The gleaming white envelope remained on the corner of Simon's desk as he rolled back his chair and stood. For Angie to come to Groves Point had taken courage. To confront him and return that damn money had cost her a lot of pride. One thing Simon remembered vividly about Angie was that she might not have had two pennies to rub together, but when it came to pride, she had been the richest lady in town.

When he'd told her to leave, she'd turned for the door and hesitated. Her small shoulders had stiffened with resolve as she refused. In that minute it was as if twelve years had been wiped out and she was seventeen again. She'd been so beautiful. And God help him, she was just as beautiful today. Naturally, several things about her were different. No longer did her silky brown hair reach her waist. Now it was shoulder length and professionally styled so that it curled around her lovely oval face.

Her graceful curves revealed a woman's body, svelte and elegant beneath a crisp, linen business suit. There had been a time when Angie hated to wear anything but washed-out jeans and faded T-shirts.

Angie had been his first love and he had been

hers. Together they had discovered the physical delights of their bodies. With excruciating patience they had held off as long as they could, because it had been so important to Angie that they be married first.

Discipline might well have been their greatest teacher. In restraining their physical desires, they had learned the delicate uses of kissing and the exquisite pleasure of exploring fingers. With a caressing gentleness they had examined every detail of foreplay until waiting a moment longer had been impossible. And then, together, their love strong and secure, they had partaken of the rhythmic ebb and flow of lovemaking. Their hearts beat as one and cried out to each other in a love so powerful that it could overtake convention, prejudice and everything else that loomed in their path.

Only it hadn't. Angie had prostituted herself. Dear God, he'd loved her so much he would have willingly given his life for her. And now he wanted to hate her with the same intensity and discovered he couldn't.

The bank was empty when Simon left his office. The envelope remained on his desk. He would do as Angie suggested, and give it to charity. Money meant little to him. He'd had it all his life and had never been happy. The only real contentment he'd ever known had been those few months with Angie. Now it seemed that she, too, had discovered money's limitations.

The Mercedes was parked in the side lot, and Simon was on Main Street before Angie drifted into his thoughts again. He wondered where she was staying and if she had come to town alone. She had used her maiden name, but he hadn't thought to look for a diamond on her ring finger. If she hadn't married, it would be a shock. One glance at the woman she had become revealed a rare jewel. Angie was a prize most men wouldn't ignore.

Engrossed in his thoughts, Simon automatically took a left turn off Main onto Oak Street on his way to the country club. Tonight he needed a long workout. A flash of color captured his attention and he glanced across the green lawn of the city park. Cindy and Bob Shannon were in the front yard firing up an antique barbecue. Dressed in blue shorts and a faded T-shirt was Angie. She sat on the Shannons' porch with a beer bottle in her hand, chatting with her friends as if she hadn't been away more than a week. Charlie Young, the school's football hero and new owner of the hardware store, came out the screen door and plopped down beside her. He said something to Angie, who threw back her head and laughed cheerfully. The musical sound of her mirth drifted through the park to Simon, assaulting him from all sides.

The muscles of his abdomen tensed. Angie was where she belonged. She was with her friends.

The sleek white Mercedes caught Angie's eye as it peeled down the narrow street. Simon. It had to be. She didn't know of anyone else in town who could afford to pay forty thousand dollars for a car. The ten thousand she'd brought was petty cash to a man like Simon, but to her it represented five years of scrimping and not building up her business as she'd wanted. Returning it was a matter of pride. She hadn't touched a dime of it. Clay had spent it chasing dreams. Her father had insisted that the Canfields owed her that money. As far as Angie was concerned, the Canfields owed her nothing.

"You have to remember we're rubbing elbows with the upper echelon," Bob teased, twisting off the cap of a beer bottle. "Ol' Charlie is now a member of the Groves Point Country Club."

"Charlie!" Cindy gave a small squeal of delight. "That's really something."

Angie thought it revealing that a city would decide Charlie unacceptable one day and welcome him the next.

"I knew there was a reason I bought that hardware store."

With the agility of a man well acquainted with the art of barbecuing, Bob flipped over the hamburgers as if he were handling hotcakes.

33

"And tell us mere serfs, your worship, what's it like to mingle with the Canfields and the Radcliffs of our fair city?"

Casually Charlie shrugged one shoulder. "Why not find out yourselves? There's a dinner tomorrow night and I'd like the three of you to come as my guests."

Cindy tossed her husband a speculative glance. "Oh, Bob, could we? I've always wanted to know what the inside of the country club looks like."

Uneasy now, Bob cleared his throat. "I suppose this means I'll have to wear a suit and tie."

"Honey, you've got the blue one we bought on sale before Easter," Cindy argued. The burst of excited happiness added a pinkish hue to her face. "Of course I'll need to have something new," she said and shared a conspiratorial smile with her friend.

Admirably, Angie refrained from laughing. From the sound of them they were all seventeen again and discussing prom night.

"What about you, Angie? Can you come?" Charlie was regarding her with an eager expression. From the minute Charlie had arrived he'd made it plain that he liked what he saw. His divorce was final, and he looked as if he was ready to try his hand at love again. In an effort to steer clear of his interest, Angie had taken pains to mention Glenn.

"Like Cindy, I'm afraid I haven't a thing to

wear," Angie explained and lifted her palm in a gesture of defeat.

"We'll both go shopping!" Cindy exclaimed with enthusiasm. "I know the perfect shop in Fairmont."

"Fairmont!" Bob choked. "Just don't go using any credit cards."

Slowly shaking her head, Cindy tossed her husband a playful look. "Robert, Robert, Robert. I've always said if the shoe fits, charge it."

Angie woke with the first light of dawn. Sunlight splashed through the open drapes and spilled over the bed and walls. Sitting up, she rubbed the sleep from her face and stood. Her watch announced that it was barely six, hardly a decent hour to be up and about on a Saturday. Cindy wasn't expecting her until ten. With four hours to kill, Angie dressed in old jeans and an Atlanta Braves T-shirt.

A truck stop on the outskirts of town was the only place open where she could get a cup of coffee. She'd hoped to avoid that area of town because the Canfields' twenty-acre property was in that direction.

As Angie climbed inside her small Ford, she realized coffee was only an excuse. Yes, she'd pull over at the truck stop, but her destination was the small clearing on the Canfield property. Something inside her needed to return there. The thought was a sad reflection of her emotional state. Twelve years had passed, and she hadn't been able to forget the love she'd shared with Simon in that small clearing in the woods. The physical aspect of their relationship still had the power to inflict a rush of regret and sorrow. They'd been wrong to steal into the church that night. Wrong to have gone against convention and the wishes of his parents. A few words whispered over her mother's Bible had never been legally binding. But Angie had felt married even if Simon hadn't.

The years had changed the land, and Angie nearly missed the turnoff from the highway. A long, sprawling house had been built, and the gravel road led to the back and a three-car garage.

Hesitating, Angie decided to ignore the house and go on. The morning was young, and it wasn't likely that she'd wake anyone. The road went deep into the property, and she could steal in and out without anyone knowing she'd ever come.

Leaving the car, Angie took care to close the door silently, not wanting the slightest sound to betray her presence. With her hands stuffed deep within her Levi's pockets, she climbed over a fallen tree and ventured into the dense forest. A gentle breeze chased a chill up her arm, but the cold wasn't from the wind. Her breathing had become shallow and uneven, and for a moment she wasn't sure she could go on. Only once had she felt this unnerved, and that had been as a child when she'd visited her mother's grave.

There were similarities. In this clearing she was returning to a time long past and a love long dead. But from the way her nerves were reacting, nothing about this time and place had been forgotten. Every tree, every limb was lovingly familiar.

To someone who didn't know these woods, the clearing would come as a surprise. The climb up the hill was steep, and just when she felt the need to pause and rest, the quiet meadow came into view. Even now, the simple beauty of this small lea caused her to stop and breathe in the morning mist. The uncomplicated elegance had been untouched by time. As she walked down the hill to the center, Angie felt like a child coming home after a long absence. The urge to hold out her arms and envelop this feeling was overwhelming. She wanted to swing around and sing, and laugh . . . and cry.

It had been here that Simon had held her in his arms and assured her that heaven and earth would pass away, but his love wouldn't. It had been here that they'd talked of the children to come and the huge house he planned to build her.

She'd laughed when he'd taken a stick and drawn out the plans in the fertile ground. They'd have lots of bedrooms and a large kitchen with plenty of cupboard space. He'd build it himself, he claimed. And remembering the skill he had with wood, Angie didn't doubt him.

Then that night in June, he had brought her to their imaginary home, lifted her in his arms and carried her over the threshold. Drunk with happiness she'd looped her arms around his neck and kissed his face until he demanded she stop.

"Just where are you taking me?" Angie had murmured, playfully nibbling on his earlobe with her teeth.

"To the master bedroom, where else, Mrs. Canfield?"

Angie tossed back her head and laughed. "Oh, Simon, I do love you. I'll make you the best wife in all South Carolina."

"I'm holding you to that," he said and kissed her until she was weak with longing. His tenderness had brought tears to her eyes as he unbuttoned her blouse and slowly slipped it from her shoulders. Her long hair fell forward as she bowed her head. Tears filled her dusky, dark eyes.

"Angie, what's wrong?"

"Nothing," she whispered. "I love you so much. It's just . . ."

"What?" Gently, he had brushed the hair from her face and kissed the corner of her eyes, stopping the flow of tears. "Angie, I'd do anything in the world for you."

"I'm being silly to cry over a silly piece of paper. I don't need it. Not when I have you. But,

Simon, do you think we'll forget our anniversary?"

"I'll never forget anything about you, or this night," he vowed. Straightening, he had taken the knife from his pocket and crossed the meadow to a huge pecan tree. It stood regal and proud, the tallest tree on the edge of the clearing. With painstaking effort he'd engraved the date and their names in the bark. The tree would stand for all time as their witness.

A distant sound of a barking dog shook Angie from her reverie. The tree. That was what was missing, gone. A broken cry filled her lungs when she located the stump. From the look of it, the tree had been crudely chopped down years ago. Simon had done this, cutting her out of his world as ruthlessly as the ax had severed the life of the mighty pecan. A hand covered her mouth to muffle the cries of pain and outrage. It shouldn't hurt this much, she told herself. But it did. The pain dug as deep as the day Simon's mother had come to her with the money.

Her legs felt as though they would no longer hold her upright, and she slumped down, sitting on the stump as the strength drained from her. Her breath came in uneven gasps and her eyes filled with stinging tears. Gone was the outrage, vanishing as quickly as it came. Her tears were those of sorrow and soulful agony. There was no more fight left in her. She had lost. Simon had appointed himself judge and divorced her with an ax. If their marriage had been a document instead of bark she at least would have had the advice of counsel. Without conscience he had cast their love aside as though it had no meaning.

A dog barked again and the sound was noticeably closer. Brushing the hair from her forehead, Angie straightened. A black Labrador raced into the clearing, barking, his tail and ears alert.

A sad smile touched Angie's eyes. "Oh, Blackie, is it really you?" Simon had trained the dog from a pup.

The angry dog ignored her, intent only in voicing his discovery.

"Blackie, don't you remember me?" Crouched as she was, Angie held out her hand for him to smell. Blackie had once been her friend as well.

"That isn't Blackie."

Simon's gruff voice from behind startled Angie. She sprang to her feet, her eyes wide and fearful as they fell on the rifle in his hands.

"This is Prince, Blackie's son." He lowered the gun at his side so that the muzzle was angled toward the ground.

Prince continued to voice his displeasure, but one sharp word from Simon silenced him.

"What happened to Blackie?"

"He died," Simon answered starkly.

"I'm sorry. . . . I know how much you . . ."

"You're trespassing."

The sun was high enough now so that it invaded the clearing, its brightness peeking through the limbs and bathing the earth with a gentle glow.

"Am I?" she asked in a voice so soft it could barely be heard. "Once it was my home."

"Don't try to make this place something it wasn't." A withdrawn look marked his features. His calm declaration chilled her more than angry words. "There was only one room here and that was the bedroom."

"Oh, Simon," she pleaded. "Don't ruin that, too."

"Too?" His intense gray eyes narrowed and a bitter laugh escaped his throat. "If anything was ruined, it was your doing, Angie."

Their gazes clashed for a long moment, and Angie swallowed back an angry retort.

"Look at us, treating each other this way." She tucked the tips of her fingers in her jeans pockets and looked past him into the clearing. There had always been a special magic to this place, a calming reassurance she hadn't found elsewhere, even in church. Here, the love they shared had sheltered and protected them from the influence of the outside world. "At one time we were best friends, and . . . and a lot more. There wasn't anything we couldn't share."

Simon tensed. "That was one hell of a long time ago." Again bitterness coated his words.

"I've hurt you, and oh, dear Simon, I'm deeply

41

sorry for that. But you need to realize that I was hurt, too. It nearly killed me to leave you and Groves Point."

"Did the money help soothe the pain?"

Stinging tears welled in her eyes, but she blinked them away, turning her hurt, questing gaze to him. She'd come to Groves Point to make her peace with Simon, but he seemed intent on lashing out at her with a storehouse of twelve years' resentment.

The curve of his mouth quirked in a derisive frown. "Tears, Angie? Believe me, I'm too old and too wise for that female trick."

Her heart wanted to cry in anguish, but no sound came from her parched throat. Proudly, she lifted her trembling chin. "It's taken me so long to come back. This place has haunted me all these years. But I never thought to find you so cold and bitter." The hard lump in her throat caused her to swallow before continuing. "I'm sorry for you, Simon. Sorry for what you've become, but I can't accept the blame." Her sweeping gaze took in the meadow, and again she was soothed by its peacefulness.

Turning away from him, she started down the steep slope toward her car. She felt Simon's presence looming above her. Proud, bitter, hurtful . . . hurting. A part of her yearned to ease that pain, but she doubted that anything she could do would touch Simon now.

Once inside the car Angie risked a look into the trees, but Simon and his dog were gone. Her hands gripped the steering wheel until the grooves made deep indentations into her palms. This wasn't the way she'd wanted things to be. Deep in her heart she'd expected to find Simon married . . . and happy.

The sudden need to escape was almost overwhelming. Glenn was right, she had needed to come back to Groves Point, but it wasn't working out as either of them had anticipated.

The turn of the car key produced a dull, grinding sound. Angie tried again. There shouldn't be anything wrong, she thought. She'd driven there without a problem. Again she tried the ignition, but only a sickly coughing sound returned.

"Oh, great." She slammed her fist against the steering wheel and groaned angrily. She didn't know a thing about the internal workings of a motor. Pulling back the hood release, she climbed out of the car. The hood was cracked open and she inserted a finger to release it fully. A full three minutes later, her finger hurt and she had yet to loosen the hood latch.

"What's the problem?" Simon's gaze impaled her, grim displeasure thinning his mouth.

"My car won't start." She felt like an idiot, standing there massaging her finger.

"Why not?"

"Go ahead, car, tell me why you won't start." She turned and mockingly questioned the Ford. "How the hell am I supposed to know? Believe me, Simon, I want out of here just as much as you want me gone."

A brittle smile cracked the hard line of his mouth. "I sincerely doubt that. Here, let me take a look." He handed the rifle to Angie. "Hold this."

Doing her best to disguise her uneasiness, Angie accepted the gun.

"It isn't loaded," he said with his back to her as he released the latch and lifted the hood. "Has this car been giving you problems?"

"No. I drove from Charleston without a hitch."

"Charleston," he repeated.

"I live there now."

The hesitation was barely noticeable. "It's a beautiful city."

Angie was holding her breath. This brief exchange was the first civil one she'd had with Simon. His dog was eyeing her again, his sleek ebony head tilted at a curious angle. Crouching down, Angie held out her hand to him a second time.

"I remember your daddy," she told him softly.

The long, black tail began to move as his cold nose smelled her fingers.

"How long have you had Prince?" Angie asked, more to carry the conversation than any desire to know the dog's age.

"Must be five, six years now." Simon's voice was muffled, his upper body folded over the side of the car. "I'm going to need a couple of tools."

"Can I get them for you?" Angie's voice was faintly high in her eagerness to help. "Believe me, car problems were the last thing I expected." She gave a small, tight laugh. "If the truth were known I was hoping to make a grand exit."

A hint of a smile touched his mouth. "My tools are in the garage."

The house had to be a good quarter mile down the gravel road.

Simon's gaze followed Angie's. "You can wait here if you prefer."

"I'd like to come with you." It felt so good to talk to Simon again without a decade of bitterness positioned between them like a brick wall. There was so much she wanted to say, and just as much she had hoped to ask. Tomorrow she'd be gone.

His gray eyes brushed over her speculatively. "If you like."

Fingertips tucked in her pockets once again, Angie matched his stride as they walked toward the house. Covertly, she studied him. The sprinkling of gray hairs at his temple gave him a distinguished look. His hair was shorter now than she recalled. But little about Simon was the way she remembered.

Her mind searched for something to say and came back empty. They were strangers. But intimate strangers. She doubted that others in this world knew Simon as well as she had at seventeen. He lived behind a stone mask now, closing himself off from the world. It hadn't taken much to discern from her conversation with Cindy and Bob that Simon had become an entity unto himself. He needed no one and had made that plain to the citizens of Groves Point.

"What do you think's wrong with my car?" she asked after a long moment, disliking the silence.

"I'm not sure."

Angie's shoes kicked up the gravel as they walked. Her usual pace was somewhat slower, but she wanted to keep even with Simon. Undoubtedly, he wanted to be rid of her as quickly as possible. But this unexpected reprieve was a welcome respite. Prince marched at his master's side, content to be with Simon, rather than run ahead.

Angie's gaze roamed over the trees and flowers that grew in abundance there. Once, years ago, she had been as young and fresh as the wildflowers, pushing through the fertile ground and seeking out the sun. Now she felt as old as the earth and not nearly as wise.

Glancing at Simon, she witnessed the proud defiance in the tilt of his head. Even the beauty of this land had been tarnished by his hate.

"I've always loved it here," she said quietly.

The subdued tone of her voice drew his gaze. "Then why did you leave?"

"Oh, Simon, if I could change our past, rectify all my mistakes, don't you think I would? I left Groves Point because I felt I was doing the best thing for us. Don't you realize that it hurt me too?"

His jaw was clenched and tight, but he said nothing as he stared unfalteringly at her.

A strained silence followed.

"Then why did you come back?"

Angie didn't know how to put into words the emotion that had driven her to Groves Point. "I wanted to return the money." An uncomplicated answer seemed best.

"You could have mailed it."

Her hand burrowed deeper into her jeans pockets. "Yes, I could have."

They approached the back of the property, giving Angie a moment to study the house. Briefly, she wondered if the interior was anything like the plans Simon had drawn for her. Excitement flashed through her and died as quickly as it sprang. Feeling the way he did about her, Simon would have gone to great lengths to avoid a house that would even faintly resemble their dream one.

"This way," Simon spoke, holding a door for her that opened into the three-car garage. The gloomy interior was filled with shadows, the open door dispersing slivers of light into the dark.

Angie's gaze fell beyond the sleek white Mercedes to the turquoise convertible.

"Simon," she whispered unsteadily as she moved into the room. "You still have the car." Reverently her hand brushed the polished fender. Some of the best times of her life had been in this old convertible. Their first kiss had taken place in this '51 Chevy. Simon had come to her house so she could help him study for a science test. Afterward he'd taken her to the A & W for a root beer. And later still, he'd nervously leaned over and lightly brushed her mouth with his. Their first kiss hadn't been much more than that, but with time their technique had greatly improved.

On countless summer evenings they'd driven up to Three Tree Point and gazed at the stars. Some evenings the heavens loomed so close that it seemed that all they had to do was reach out and pluck the stars from the sky. Simon had cradled her in his arms and whispered that if it were in his power, he'd weave moonbeams as a crown for her hair.

"I've been meaning to sell that old thing for years," he said flatly. "It doesn't run and hasn't in years. All it does it take up space in the garage."

Angie dropped her hand to her side. "It brings back a lot of memories." The corners of her mouth lifted with a sad smile.

He didn't speak for a minute. "Yes, I suppose it does," he said as though the thought hadn't occurred to him.

Simon would like her to think the old Chevy convertible was a useless piece of junk, but Angie wasn't easily fooled. There had been too many hot summer days when she'd helped him smear the car wax over a spotless surface, her reflection shining like glass from the polished hood. Simon loved this old car. The fact that it was in his garage said as much.

"I'm ready to go." His eyes had narrowed into silver slits as he paused at the door, toolbox in hand. "Are you coming or not?"

Reluctantly, Angie left the car. She would have liked to look inside the glove compartment, to see what secrets it held.

They were several yards down the road before Simon spoke again. "How's Clay?"

The question surprised her. Clay and Simon had never been close. They had tolerated each other. Clay's dislike of the Canfields had been as strong as Simon's distrust of her now. "He's doing well," she said and didn't elaborate.

Simon breathed in deeply. "What about you, Angie, are you happy?"

Her throat went dry and a bubble of hysterical laughter choked off a reply. For twelve years her life had been in limbo. Could anyone be content there? She hadn't thought about being happy, not really not in years. Happiness was relative to her circumstances. "I suppose."

"You must enjoy Charleston, it's a beautiful city."

Each question was a gentle prod. He cared enough to be curious and that pleased her. "I own a flower shop."

Simon nodded, seemingly unsurprised. "You always did love flowers. Business must be good." He was referring to the envelope she'd given him.

She lifted one shoulder in a delicate shrug. "I can't complain."

Idly she picked up a stick and threw it for Prince. Playing catch had been Blackie's favorite game, and his son was sure to appreciate it, too. Immediately the Labrador kicked up his feet and shot into the woods. Angie's musical laughter followed him.

Simon stopped and studied her, their gazes clashing. "Your laugh is the same."

Angie dropped her eyes first. "I wouldn't like to think much about me was different."

"Why not? We all change in twelve years."

"That's not what I meant." She wasn't quite sure what she was trying to explain. Simon was right, there were several things different about her. She was a mature woman now, not a naive teenager.

Proudly, Prince returned with the stick, and

bending over to retrieve it gave Angie a moment to compose her thoughts. "In some ways, I'm looking to recapture that enchanted summer of my life. That summer with you."

"You can't." Simon's words cut at her as painfully as a slashing knife. "That time is gone forever."

Angie paused and felt a compelling urge to reach out and touch him. Tightening her hand around the stick, Angie threw it again. "I know."

"Why did you come back?" Simon demanded harshly. "Why now, after all this time?"

Slowly, she turned toward him. "I had to come, I've wasted too many years as it is."

Panting, Prince returned with the stick, but when Angie bent over to take it from his mouth Simon stopped her. Gripping her left hand he raised his eyes to hers.

His dark brows furrowed together. "You've never married?"

Angie swallowed, but her voice wavered emotionally. "I couldn't. I married at seventeen."

❧ Three ❧

Simon went pale, his hand dropping hers. "Are you saying that you never married because of what we did?"

Her head drooped. Angie couldn't find the words to explain. "No. I realized when your mother gave me the check that whatever commitment you felt toward me was over."

"Haven't you got that turned around?"

"How do you mean?" Angie asked, missing the gist of his question. She remembered vividly how Georgia Canfield had come to her and explained that Simon had found another girl at college.

"I wasn't the one who asked to be free." His mouth tightened grimly.

"Not technically," she argued. "You sent your mother to do it for you."

"What?" he exploded. He opened his mouth, then closed it again as if to cut off what he was about to say. "I think we'd better talk." Pivoting sharply, he headed toward the house, leaving a confused Angie to follow in his wake.

He was so far ahead of her that by the time she reached the back of the house, he was already inside and the door was left open, waiting for her.

The back door led to a porch with a matching

washer and dryer. Angie wiped the mud from her shoes on the braided rug just inside. Rounding the corner she paused in the doorway of the kitchen. The room was huge with bright counter-tops and shining appliances. Apparently, Simon had someone come in to do the housekeeping.

His hip was leaning against the long counter, his arms crossed over his chest. "Now say that again?"

"What? That your mother asked for your freedom?"

"Yes." His eyes were measuring her with an accusing glint. "How could you have believed such a thing?" He looked as if he wanted to strangle her.

"I didn't!" she shouted in her defense. "Don't you remember I took the Greyhound bus to the university. I asked you myself."

"By God, you couldn't have." He straightened and began pacing the polished tile floor like a tormented beast trapped in the close confines of a cage. Suddenly, as if he needed to sit down, he pulled out a chair. "I think we had better start at the beginning."

Angie joined him at the round oak table, her hands clasped in her lap. The confrontation with his mother might have taken place twelve years ago, but she vividly remembered it as if it had happened yesterday. And now Simon was acting as if none of this were true.

"Don't lie to me, Simon. Not now, after all these years."

"I swear before everything I hold dear that I never asked to be free from you, Angie." Every facet of his face was intent, imploring.

Slowly, Angie shook her head, not knowing what to believe.

"Start from the beginning," he urged, his gray eyes wide and rapt.

"You'd left for the university that September."

He nodded. "I wrote to you practically every day and phoned almost that often. How could you have possibly believed there was someone else?"

Her nails cut painfully into her palms. She couldn't deny that in the beginning he'd contacted her daily. Being separated like that had been miserable for them both. But Simon seemed to have adjusted more quickly than she. "At first you did."

"What does that mean?" His eyes narrowed defensively.

"I . . . noticed that around November your letters became less frequent." She lowered her eyes to the quilted placemat on the tabletop. "You didn't phone nearly as often either."

"I was saving money so I could buy you a Christmas present. The phone bill for October had taken nearly all my allowance."

She had known that, too. But at the time, she'd been so unhappy without him that every day apart had seemed an eternity. "I knew you were involved with basketball so I didn't say anything. But whenever we talked, you were always in such a hurry, and even your letters were getting shorter and shorter."

"Dear God, Angie, I was about to flunk out of two classes because I spent so much time writing and talking to you."

It all sounded so petty now. She wanted to tear her eyes away from him but found she couldn't. His smoldering gaze held her captive, demanding that she continue.

"The second week in February your mother came into the pharmacy and said she needed to talk to me." Nervously her fingers toyed with the fringe around the orange-and-brown plaid placemat. "She . . . she said that she'd noticed over the holidays that you were unhappy." This was hard, so much harder than she had ever imagined it could possibly be. Each word was wrenched from her until her voice wavered on an audible tremor. "She said you'd found another girl at school, but you felt guilty about me. She didn't want me to be hurt and offered me the . . . money to leave town."

Simon's hand reached for hers, gripping it so tightly that it felt as though he had cut off the flow of blood to her fingers. "Angie, I hadn't."

Tears shimmered in her eyes and she bit into the corner of her bottom lip. "I didn't want to believe her. That's why I took the bus to see you. If you were going to be rid of me, then you'd have to tell me yourself."

Leaning his elbow on the table, Simon wiped a hand over his bloodless features and pinched the bridge of his nose. "You were walking in front of the fraternity." Simon's own memory of that last meeting was strikingly clear. Her long, shining dark hair had been tied back and her mournful, troubled eyes had searched his. He had known she needed him at that moment, but couldn't stand the pressure of another demand.

"I'd been waiting outside your fraternity for an hour, pacing," Angie inserted, caught in her own reminiscence. "I wanted so badly to believe it wasn't true. But you took one look at me and said you hoped to God I wasn't pregnant. A pregnancy would ruin everything."

Simon turned his head and stared out the kitchen window with unseeing eyes. That day had to have been the worst of his life. His grades had been so poor that he was kicked off the basketball team. He'd found Angie after leaving the coach's office, where he'd gotten the lecture of his life. His father had been to the university earlier that week, berating him. The last thing he needed was to have Angie show up and tell him she was pregnant.

"And you assumed from what my mother said that everything was true."

"It made sense at the time," she murmured, the tremble in her low voice barely noticeable any longer. "It had been weeks since you'd seen me and when you did, you acted like . . ."

"I know how I acted." Rising to his feet, Simon crossed the room, jerked out a drawer and fumbled with a pack of cigarettes. His fingers shook as he lit one. Inhaling deeply, he aimed the smoke at the ceiling. "So you returned to Groves Point, took the money and moved out of town."

She hadn't wanted that ten thousand dollars. Clay was the one who'd insisted they take it. Simon owed her that much, he had argued. All Angie had cared about was the desperate need to escape Groves Point, and the Canfields. "Yes, I took the money and left." She offered no excuses. None were needed.

"So much for trust and vows spoken before God." His attitude was flippant as he viciously ground out the half-smoked cigarette in a glass ashtray.

Tears stung the back of her eyes. This wasn't a time for accusations, but for understanding and forgiving. In her hurt anger she lashed back at him with a vengeance. "I notice it didn't take you long to seek solace." Her nerves felt threadbare. "How many women warmed your blood before you married Carol?"

Savagely, Simon raked his fingers through his dark hair. "Three years, Angie. For three years I waited for you to come back." His mouth was pinched, the bracketing grooves, white.

He'd waited for her to return. Shock waves rippled over her as her eyes widened in painful astonishment. An involuntary sob filled her throat, and she cupped her mouth to muffle the tormented sound of her cry. "Even when I'd taken the money, you waited?" Blinking back the ready flow of emotion, she stared up at him. "Oh, Simon . . ."

He took a step toward her and paused uncertainly. If he touched her, he wasn't sure he'd ever be able to let her go again. A myriad of emotions raged through him like a wildfire on a sun-scorched field. Anger. Surprise. Regret. But paramount was a burning sense of betrayal by the ones he loved and trusted most.

Impulsively, Angie raised her hand and reached out, lightly touching his forearm. Moisture shimmered in her eyes as she raised her gaze to him.

He caught her hand and gripped it as though it were a lifeline to sanity. "Angie, dear God, how could we have let this happen to us?"

"I don't know," she whispered, her voice wavering and unsteady. "It was all so long ago."

"I could kill them."

"No, no, don't even think such a thing." Vaulting to her feet, she forcefully shook her head. "There's been enough hate and misunderstanding. Your parents did what they thought was best for you."

The pinched look about his mouth didn't relax. "They had no right—"

"No, they didn't," she agreed readily. "But who's to say what the future held for us? We were both incredibly young. . . ."

"And stupid," Simon inserted. "But it doesn't change what they did."

The cold ruthlessness was back in Simon. At seventeen she'd never seen that side of him. Their world had been filled with high ideals and warm promises. Who could have said that their love would last more than a year?

"I'm leaving in the morning," she said softly, her hand reaching for his and clasping it tightly. "And when I do I want to look back on these past few days as a healing time in my life. I came back to Groves Point to make my peace, not to stir up grief. I bear no one malice, least of all your family. We need to forgive your parents and my dad. But most of all, we need to forgive each other."

Simon expelled an angry breath as his gaze narrowed on her upturned face. "I don't know that I can," he ground out. Without warning he reached for her, bringing her into the tight circle of his arms.

Having Simon hold her like this was like returning safely home after fighting a twelve-year

59

battle. With her ear pressed against his chest, she heard the steady drumbeat of his heart. He released a sigh of contentment and she felt him rub his unshaved chin across the crown of her head. They had shared the most beautiful part of their youth together. Simon would always be someone special in her life, but the love they shared was over. She was free now. Free to return to Charleston and Glenn. Free to love.

A surge of happiness brought an excited bubble of laughter from her throat. "I'm so relieved."

"I don't know what I feel," he confessed in a strained voice. All the emotions remained, most of which he would need to deal with privately. But Angie was here, in his arms, and he had to find a way to keep her there. "Angie," he murmured her name as he loosened his grip. A hand on each of her shoulders pushed her gently back so he could study her. Lord, she was beautiful. Even her tear-streaked face couldn't mar the natural beauty of her perfect features. The lovely mouth drew his attention, and he struggled to align his thoughts. "I don't want you to leave tomorrow." Not when he'd just found her again. Not when he'd been offered a second chance at life. Holding Angie was like stepping into the freshness of a newborn spring after suffering through the bitter cold of winter.

Angie was stunned. Simon's asking her to remain in Groves Point was the last thing she'd expected. "I have to go. My home, my business . . . everything's in Charleston." Suddenly it was vitally important that she get back to Glenn. There was so much she was burning to tell him.

"Stay longer—only a few more days," he pleaded, his fingers tightening their grip on the slender curve of her shoulders. "Just until we have things worked out."

"I can't." Her eyes implored him to understand. She was afraid of what would develop if she did. Simon and Groves Point were a part of her life that belonged in the past. Glenn and Charleston were her future. "In fact," she murmured, glancing at her wristwatch, "I need to be leaving right away. Cindy's expecting me." It was on the tip of her tongue to mention that she'd be at the country club dance that evening. But it wasn't an event she was looking forward to attending.

"Your car." Simon straightened as his gaze shifted to the tools lying on the top of the counter. A near-smile touched his mouth. "Since we're speaking honestly here, I guess I should own up. I pulled your hot wire."

"My what?" Angie stared up at him blankly.

"Your car. That's why it wouldn't start."

She was flabbergasted. "But why?" She'd have thought he would have gone to any lengths to be rid of her.

"I didn't know the car was yours when I did it.

If someone was trespassing on my property, I didn't want them running off until I knew the reason."

"Oh." The logic in that was irrefutable.

"And later, when I discovered it was you—" he paused and smiled wryly "—I was happy to have an excuse for you to stay."

"I'm so glad you did," she admitted, keeping her voice low.

By unspoken agreement they left the kitchen, walking into the sunlight that shone down on them like a healing balm.

His hand rested lightly at the base of her neck as if he needed to touch her. How different their steps on this same bit of road had been only a short time ago.

Simon repaired her car within minutes by simply reconnecting the wire. When he lowered the hood, an awkward silence hung between them.

After wiping his fingers clean on a white handkerchief, Simon stuffed it in his back pocket. "I want to see you again."

Her heart was going crazy, its beat accelerating to an alarming rate. Part of her was crying out to explore the unbelievable tenderness they had once shared. Maybe if so much time hadn't elapsed, she would have been more willing. But the worlds that separated them twelve years ago had widened even more. She couldn't come back.

Her eyes were sad when they met his. She was angry because he asked and angry because she knew what her answer must be. "I'm sorry, so sorry, but no."

He looked for a moment as if he didn't believe her. "Why not?"

"Because what we shared was a long time ago. We can't recapture our youth. Nor can we alter the past. The time has come to go on."

His brow furrowed in a thick frown, Simon shook his head, and captured her hand with his. "Angie, listen to me. I love you. I can live a hundred years and never feel this strongly about another woman."

"Simon, don't," she pleaded, feeling guilty and increasingly miserable. "What you love is a memory."

"No," he argued with a warm gentleness that nearly undid her. "I love *you*."

"You don't know me," she shouted desperately in a half sob, reaching inside the car for her purse. Her fingers fumbled with the clasp, as she struggled to remove her car keys.

"I'm not going to push this." His fingertips brushed a stray tear from her ashen cheek. A dry grin twisted his mouth. "But I think it's a sad commentary on our lives if, after twelve years, you suggest we need more time."

Angie's laugh escaped on the swell of a broken sob. "You're going to start me crying all over again. Oh, Lord, Simon. I've cried more these past few days than I have in years."

"Good," he murmured, taking a step closer, "let those tears be an absolution." He placed his hand on the gentle curve of her neck, his long fingers sliding into the silken length of her hair. His other hand wiped the moisture from her cheek. Unhurried, his mouth made a slow descent to her trembling lips.

As the distance lessened, Angie closed her eyes. She should break away, she thought guiltily, but the curiosity to discover his kiss again was overpowering. They weren't teenagers anymore, but adults, curious after a long absence.

His lips warmly covered hers, his touch firm and experienced. The tension eased from Angie as she slid her hands over his rib cage, feeling his hard muscles through the material of his shirt.

The pulse point in her neck throbbed against his fingers, betraying his overwhelming effect on her. Her hold tightened as her mouth clung to his.

"Oh, Simon," she whispered as his mouth released her.

Slowly he lifted his head, awed by the power an uncomplicated kiss held over him. Angie's eyes were wide and faintly puzzled. This overpowering response was just as much of a surprise to her. She resembled a frightened doe, unsure of her footing. His first reaction was to reach out and hold her secure. But he couldn't.

As difficult as it was at this moment, he had to let her go. In some ways, it had been easier the first time. He dropped his hands to his side and took a step in retreat.

"Goodbye, Simon," she said in a choked, unhappy voice.

He couldn't answer her. For him the kiss wasn't a farewell, but a welcoming. He opened the car door for her and closed it once she'd climbed inside.

The car engine roared to life without a problem. Her eyes glistened with tears as Angie shifted the gears, backed the car around and drove away. Not once did she glance in her rearview mirror, although everything within her was demanding that she take one last look at Simon.

A blazing orange sun was greeting the horizon when the two couples pulled into the country club parking lot.

"I'm as nervous as a virgin on her wedding night," Cindy confessed as Bob gave her his hand and helped her out of the back seat of Charlie's Lincoln Continental.

"How do I look?" Cindy nervously asked Angie as her fingers brushed at a small crease in the front of her dove-gray silk dress.

"Gorgeous," Angie said and winked. "We both do." After spending the morning and most of the afternoon shopping she wouldn't admit to anything else. Cindy did look lovely. Even Bob's jaw had dropped in surprise when his wife had appeared.

Bob inserted a finger in the starched white collar of his shirt. "Are you sure there isn't going to be a problem?" His question was directed at Charlie.

"I'm sure," Charlie returned confidently. "Everyone's entitled to bring guests."

As he'd promised, there wasn't so much as a raised eyebrow as they entered the foyer. Charlie signed in for them, and with a hand cupping Angie's elbow, he led the way into the dining room.

Each round table was covered with a pure-white linen tablecloth. An expertly folded red napkin was standing at attention at each place setting. The lights had been lowered and flickering candles cast a festive glow across the room. The hardwood dance floor was toward the front, and the band instruments were set up and waiting.

Cindy was whispering excitedly to Bob, who was walking behind Angie, but she couldn't hear her friend. Perhaps she would have been more in awe of the fancy club if Simon hadn't brought her here all those years ago. Once for a birthday dinner, and again for a dance. But his parents had objected strenuously to Simon taking Angie to the club. They had fought, and Angie, not wishing to be a source of problems for Simon at home, had refused to come again.

Charlie pulled out the high-backed chair for

Angie, and Bob followed suit. The two women exchanged happy smiles.

"I guess I have to come to the country club for Bob to pull out my chair," Cindy teased her husband affectionately.

Within minutes they were studying an oblong menu, a gold tassel hanging from the top.

The women ordered veal picatta and the men chose steak au poivre. Charlie insisted on paying for their meal, but Bob picked up the tab for the domestic wine, a delicious Chardonnay.

Nostalgia flowed as freely as the wine, and an hour later while they lingered over freshly brewed coffee, the five-piece band started up.

Only a few couples took to the floor.

"Do you dance, Angie?" Charlie leaned toward her and asked.

"It's been a while," she admitted. Her life-style didn't take in many evenings like this one. She and Glenn shared many quiet evenings alone, but he was a lumberjack of a man and had never suggested they go dancing.

"My feet are itching already," Cindy confessed and pointedly batted her curved lashes at her husband.

As Angie recalled, Bob and Cindy made quite a couple on the dance floor. They proved her memory correct as they took to the floor with an ease that produced a sigh of admiration from Angie.

"Shall we?" Charlie held out his hand to her.

"Why not?" Angie answered with a warm smile. "But forgive me if I step on your toes. It's been a long time."

"I'll come up with some penance," Charlie teased, drawing her into his arms when they reached the outskirts of the floor.

Angie felt stiff and a little awkward as Charlie tightened his hold. "You're still as beautiful as ever," he whispered. "I always thought you were the prettiest girl in class."

Angie managed to hide a soft smile. Charlie had dated a long succession of cheerleaders. In four years of high school, she doubted that he'd ever given her more than a second glance.

"You were dating Canfield and he let it be known in no uncertain terms that you were his."

A part of her would always be Simon's, Angie mused, a thoughtful frown creasing her brow. She didn't want to have to think about Simon.

"You've done well for yourself, Charlie." Early in the evening, Angie had realized that Charlie enjoyed talking about his success. It was easier to listen to self-proclaimed accolades than discuss her relationship with Simon.

The music was slow, and as they turned Angie caught sight of a silver-haired woman with delicate features sitting at a table against the window. Georgia Canfield, Simon's mother. Angie's heart stopped cold. The older woman had changed dramatically. In twelve years, she'd aged thirty. One look confirmed that life hadn't been easy for Simon's mother and a rush of unexpected compassion filled Angie. She had often wondered what she'd feel if she saw Mrs. Canfield again. The bitterness had been with her a lot of years, just as it had been with Simon.

"Excuse me a minute," she said as she broke loose from Charlie. "There's someone I'd like to see."

Charlie dropped his arms, surprised. "Sure."

Making her way across the crowded dance floor, Angie formulated her thoughts. This was possibly the worst thing she could do, but the opportunity was here and she wouldn't allow it to escape.

"Hello, Mrs. Canfield," she spoke softly as she stood before the older woman who was sitting alone at the small table.

A network of wrinkles broke out across her face as she turned, unable to disguise her shock. "Angela."

"I hope you'll forgive me for being so brash as to intrude on you this evening."

"All young people are brash," Mrs. Canfield said, recovering quickly. "What are you doing here? As I recall, my husband and I paid a steep price to keep you out of this town."

Angie's fingers laced in front of her, tightened. "I realize that. I've only come for a visit."

"I didn't know you had relatives in the area," Mrs. Canfield said stiffly.

"I haven't." Angie eyed the empty chair across from Simon's mother. "Would you mind if I sat down? I'd like to talk for a moment."

Georgia Canfield answered with a polite nod, but Angie noted that her shoulders were arched and her back was uncomfortably straight.

"I won't stay long," Angie promised as she took the seat. Her insides were tied in a double knot, but she knew she appeared outwardly calm, as did Mrs. Canfield. "First, I want to ask your forgiveness for taking that money. There hasn't been a day since that I haven't regretted it."

Gray eyes, so like Simon's, widened perceptively.

"By accepting your offer," Angie continued relentlessly, "I confirmed every bad thing you wanted to believe about me."

"I realized at the time that it was more your father's doing than yours."

"That's no excuse." Both were aware that Clay Robinson was a weak man, but Angie refused to lessen the blame on herself.

"Have you seen Simon?" Georgia Canfield gave no indication that she was concerned, and Angie marveled at her composure.

"Yes, I talked to him at the bank yesterday when I returned the money."

"Returned the money . . ." The piercing eyes

held Angie's for a long moment. "Are you planning to move back?"

An intense sadness settled over Angie. Simon's mother was more concerned that she was going to intrude on their lives. The fact they might discover her subterfuge didn't appear to concern her.

"No," she answered simply. "I'll be leaving town in the morning."

The older woman looked relieved. "It was good to see you again, Angela. Although you may think differently, I do wish you well."

Their eyes met and held over the top of the table. "I bear you no ill will," Angie said and, placing her hand against the edge of the table, stood. "Goodbye, Mrs. Canfield."

The silver-haired woman lowered her gaze first. "Goodbye, Angela."

Angie inserted the key into her apartment door, turned the latch and reached inside for the switch. A flood of light filled the room. She blinked and lowered her suitcase to the floor. Charleston seemed a different world from Groves Point. Here there was an elegance and grace that had all but vanished from the rest of the South, or at least what she'd seen of it.

The phone drew her gaze and Angie eagerly crossed the room to punch out Glenn's number.

"Glenn," she said, barely giving him time to answer. "Listen to me."

His husky laugh met her. "Angie, of course I'll listen to you. Are you back?"

"Yes, yes, I just walked in the door and I'm dying to see you."

"I'm on my way, Babe."

The phone clicked in her ear, and with a sigh of contentment, Angie carried her suitcase into her bedroom. The trip across town would take Glenn a good twenty minutes; she would have time to shower and look her best.

The doorbell chimed exactly eighteen minutes later and she crossed the floor quickly, flinging open the door. "Glenn," she whispered, "oh, Glenn." She reached for him, faintly aware that he was taller and more muscular than Simon. Her arms slid around his neck as she met his mouth in a fierce kiss.

With his arms wrapped around her waist, Glenn lifted her from the carpet and swung her around, closing the door with the heel of his shoe.

"If that's the kind of warm welcome I get, I just may send you away more often."

"And I'd go." Angie smiled up into dark eyes. Glenn was a dear, dear man. There were few in all the world whom she trusted more. He wasn't handsome, not in the way Simon was. His brow was wide and intelligent, his mouth a little too full and his nose a trifle too pronounced. But at this moment, Angie couldn't recall a man more wonderful.

"Glenn, dear, sweet Glenn." Leaning back, she held both his hands with her own. "You've asked me this question a hundred times and finally I can answer you."

The teasing, happy glint left his eyes and Angie watched as they grew dark and intense.

"Yes, Glenn, I'll marry you."

 Four

With Prince trotting at his side, Simon rounded the last curve in the road that led him back to the house. The sun was rising, bathing the earth in the golden light of early morning. Sweat rolled off Simon's face as a surge of energy carried him the last quarter mile.

Just inside the gravel driveway Simon paused, his hands on his knees as he leaned forward and dragged deep gulps of oxygen into his heaving lungs. He hated these early morning runs and did them only as a means of self-discipline. But this morning had been different. With every foot that pounded the pavement, he filled his mind with thoughts of Angie. For the first time in more years than he cared to remember, his thoughts of her weren't tainted with bitterness. Unbridled, his mind roamed freely over their early days and the little things that had attracted him to her. His heart hammered and with every beat it repeated her name: Angie, Angie, Angie. He remembered the first time he'd ever really noticed her. She'd been standing by her locker in their high school, laughing with a friend. Her long straight hair had reached her waist and shone as if blessed by a benevolent sun god. The musical sound of her laughter had caught him by surprise, and he paused to see what was so amusing. His gaze had found hers and the feelings he had experienced when he viewed this slim dark-haired girl had enthralled him. This was a girl from Oak Street. Simon hadn't even been sure he remembered her name.

From that moment on, he began to notice little things about Angela Robinson. His classmates often sought her out, pausing to say a few words to her on their way to class. Her smile had a way of lighting up her entire face. Her eyes were the darkest shade of brown he'd ever seen, a mysterious deep color. The girls came to her with their problems, knowing Angie was never too busy to listen. Even the guys set her aside in their minds. Subtly Simon had tried to find out what he could about her and discovered that where the guys were usually loose-tongued about girls, they weren't about Angie. Even his best friend, Cal Spencer, seemed reluctant to talk about her.

"What do you want to know for?" Cal had insisted.

"I hadn't noticed her before, that's all. Is she new?" Simon knew she wasn't. Faintly he could recall seeing her there sophomore year.

"No. She's been around a while."

"Who's she dating?" Simon pressed.

"Hey, man, she's a nice kid, leave her alone. Okay?"

Cal's words had irritated Simon. Damn, what

did he care anyway? he had thought. This girl who had captured his attention lived on Oak Street. Hell, she wasn't even that pretty. Not in the way Shirley Radcliff was, and he'd been dating her for weeks. The way things were going he'd be sleeping with Shirley by summer. Most of the guys had already been laid and took pride in recounting their experiences. Simon was sixteen and he felt it was high time he shared his own conquests.

"If you must know," Cal cut in abruptly, "Angie looked over my term paper before I handed it in to that old biddy Carson."

"You mean she wrote it for you, don't you?" Simon teased, nudging his friend with an elbow.

"No. I offered to pay her, but she refused. She said that she'd be happy to help, but she wouldn't do it for me."

"Did she?"

"Yeah, and she's helped me and a lot of the others having trouble, too."

"What do you mean?" Simon didn't like the sound of that.

"She's got brains and isn't a snob about it."

From then on, Simon had found that he watched her even more. Angie wasn't the cheerleader type, nor was she outgoing and vivacious. But she was the heart of their junior class. She was loved and respected, and there wasn't a person in all Groves Point High who had a bad thing to say about her. It wasn't that Simon was attracted to her. He had Shirley. But he was captivated by this long-haired girl with the shy smile and the warm heart. The longer he studied her the more he realized that people were comfortable around her. Nothing about her was manufactured.

It had taken Simon a week to gather up enough courage to approach Angie. He had started by passing her in the hall and talking to her as if he'd been doing it for years. "Hello, Angie."

The first time she had looked shocked. "Hi . . ." It hadn't occurred to him that she might not know his name. Everyone knew the Canfields.

Other meetings, supposedly by accident, followed. He had just happened to be driving by one day when she was walking home from school alone.

"Hi." He pulled his shining turquoise convertible to the curb and looped an arm over the seat. "I'm going your way. Can I give you a lift?"

Angie had tucked a piece of hair around her ear and shaken her head. "No, thanks, it's only a few blocks."

Her refusal vexed him. This was Simon Canfield she had just turned down. The boy who scored the most points on the basketball team, son of the banker, and the richest kid in town. Who the hell did she think she was anyway?

Another week passed before Simon approached her again. This time they both were in the city library. Simon played it cool and didn't say a word. He did, however, nod in her direction once when he had caught her eye. She smiled in return and glanced down at her books.

Simon picked up a book on archeology and sat at the table across from her. For a full twenty minutes neither said a word. Simon pretended to be reading, but his gaze was drawn unwillingly to her several times. The feeling of being this close to her was euphoric. But for all the attention she gave him, he thought, he might as well have been a pillar of salt.

Even now he couldn't remember who spoke first. What he did recall was that they sat and talked until the library closed. Simon discovered that he loved to hear Angie speak. Her voice was low and melodic. It wasn't her voice so much as what she said; her insights were refreshing. She made him feel intelligent and awakened a sense of humor in him he'd never known he possessed. He liked Shirley and had even thought he loved her, but after an hour with Angie he found Shirley utterly boring.

Although it was dark when they left the library, Angie again insisted on walking home. Simon remembered that he tried to sound casual about meeting her again sometime and had even made an excuse about needing help with one of his subjects. Undoubtedly she saw through that. He was an honor student himself.

After that they met nightly at the public library. With each meeting, Simon tasted a little more of the secret beauty that attracted Angie to his friends. She was lovely without being beautiful. Intelligent without being shrewd. And shy without being docile.

At school she smiled at him in the halls, but never sought him out. Since they didn't share any classes, Simon had to go out of his way to see her. He did so willingly, not caring who saw him or what they said.

Two weeks after he first started meeting Angie at the library, Shirley announced that she'd decided to start seeing another guy. If she'd expected Simon to argue, she was disappointed. Actually Simon was grateful. He wanted to ask Angie to the dance after the game Friday night and would have felt obligated to Shirley.

Angie turned him down flat.

For two nights he didn't show up at the library. Nor did he make a point of passing her in the halls. He wasn't stupid; he'd gotten the message.

The Wednesday before the game, Simon stayed after school shooting baskets in the basketball hoop beside the tennis courts. Almost everyone had gone home. He didn't know how long he had continued to drive to the hoop . . . long after his muscles had protested the exercise . . . long after his throat felt dry and his stomach ached . . . long after Angie had walked over to watch him.

Even when he did notice her, he pretended he hadn't.

"Simon."

"Yeah." He continued bouncing the ball, took aim and shot from the free-throw line. The ball swished through the net.

"About the dance . . ."

Bouncing the ball, Simon drowned out her words, shot, missed, made a rebound and slam-dunked the basketball.

"Simon . . . I . . ." she hesitated, and her voice became small.

He tucked the ball under his arm and wiped the sweat from his face with the back of his hand. "Listen, I got the picture. You don't want to go to the dance with me. Fine, there are plenty of other girls who would jump at the chance." His throat felt as dry as sandpaper. Without a backward glance he walked to the water fountain and drank enough to ease the parched feel.

Angie followed him. "Would you consider taking me if—" she swallowed "—if I met you there?"

"Met you there?" Simon repeated, astonished. "Listen, Angie, I know you live on Oak Street. I do drive in that part of town. It isn't any crime to live where you do."

"I know, it's just that my dad, well . . . Would it be all right if I met you at the gym?"

"No," he repeated calmly, "it wouldn't be all

right. If I ask a girl out then I expect to pick her up and take her home. Understand?"

Slowly Angie nodded. Her arms tightened around her books, crushing them to her chest. "That's the kind of thing you should do."

"Are you coming with me or not?" Simon shifted his weight to his left foot, the basketball tucked under his arm. He tried to give the appearance that it didn't matter to him either way. If she went with him, fine. If not, he'd ask another girl. The choice was hers.

"Thank you for asking me, Simon. I'll always remember that you did." With that she turned and walked away.

A long minute passed before Simon ran after her. "Angie."

She hesitated before turning around. Her face was so pale that her dark eyes were in sharp contrast to her bloodless features. "Yes."

She looked so miserable that he immediately wanted to comfort her. "I could pick you up at the library."

"Would you?" Her voice grew even softer.

"I don't want to go to the dance with anyone but you."

She looked for a moment as if she wanted to cry. Biting her lower lip, she gnawed on it before forcing a smile. "There's no one else I'd want to take me."

"Can I carry your books?"

She nodded and when he reached for her hand she gave him that, too.

That night they'd shared a tentative kiss. For the first time Angie let Simon drive her home from the library. They stopped at the local drive-in for something to drink, and sat and talked until Angie glanced at her watch and looked startled. She had Simon drop her off a block before Oak Street. Her fingers were on the doorknob when Simon stopped her by placing a hand on her shoulder. Surprised, she looked back. Simon said nothing as he leaned forward and gently brushed his mouth over hers. He'd experienced far more passionate kisses, but none so sweet.

By the time he arrived home, Simon was whistling.

"You've got it bad," Cal had commented a month later.

"What do you mean?" Simon decided to play dumb.

"You and Angela Robinson."

"Yeah, so what's the big deal? She's terrific, I like her."

"I like Angie too. Everyone does, but you know what kind of problem you'll face if you ask her to the prom."

Simon did know. Hell, it had been in his mind all week. Angie hadn't mentioned it, but the biggest dance of the year loomed before them like D Day. For all his parents knew he was still dating Shirley. Neither his mother nor his father would appreciate him asking a girl from Oak Street to the country club dinner scheduled for after the prom. For that matter, Angie had never mentioned her home or family, either.

They'd continued to see each other nightly, with Simon dropping her off a block from Oak Street and sitting in the car until she was safely inside her house. A couple of times he'd driven down her street without her knowing it and had been surprised at how meticulous the yard and flower beds were. As far as he could see there was nothing to be ashamed of. He worried about Angie and wondered if her father was abusive or alcoholic. She had given him no clues, but he couldn't press the subject, since he hadn't taken her to meet his parents, either.

A week before the dance Simon had made his decision. "We're going," he announced that night. They were parked at Three Tree Point, sitting in the convertible with the top down. Angie sat close to his side, her head resting on his chest. Simon's arm was looped around her shoulder and he pressed her close.

Angie hadn't made the pretense of not knowing what he was talking about. "There'll be trouble."

"We'll face it together." Slowly, reassuringly, his hand stroked the length of her arm. "And this time I won't pick you up at the library or anyplace else. I'm coming to your front door with the biggest corsage this town has ever seen."

"Oh, Simon," she had whispered, uncertainty in her voice, "I don't know."

"And with you on my arm, I'm going to introduce you proudly to my parents."

Simon felt the tension building in her. "You're sure?"

"I've never been more positive of anything in my life."

The evening had been a disaster from beginning to end. As he said he would, Simon picked up Angie at her house. He had barely knocked when the door was opened. Simon wasn't sure what he expected, but it wasn't the tall, gray-haired man who stood before him. Simon introduced him-self and shook hands with Angie's father, Clay Robinson. Clay was dressed in a suit, his hair slicked down. From listening around school, Simon knew that Angie's father worked at the mill. Weekends he played banjo at a local tavern.

"You've come to take my Angie to the prom?"

"Yes, sir."

"You're that rich kid from on the hill, ain't you?"

"Yes, sir."

"I don't suppose you and your daddy like good bluegrass?"

"Daddy, please," Angie pleaded, her face red with embarrassment.

"We enjoy music." All Simon wanted to do was get Angie out that house.

"Me and my band play good, you say something to your daddy, you hear, boy?"

"Yes, sir."

Angie didn't say a word until Simon had parked the car in the parking lot. The music drifted from the open door of the school gymnasium. "I'm sorry, Simon," she mumbled, her chin tucked against her collarbone.

"What for?"

"Dad. He shouldn't have asked you to do that."

"Angie, it doesn't matter. Okay?" A finger under her chin lifted her eyes to his. They were so dark and intense that he leaned forward and kissed her. "Have I told you how beautiful you are tonight?" She was, incredibly so. Her hair was piled high upon her head, and small flowers were woven into the design. The dress was new, a light blue thing with an illusion yoke of sheer lace. Angie had designed it herself and he was astonished at her skill.

For the first time that evening, she smiled. "No."

"Then let me correct the oversight." He chuckled. "You are incredibly beautiful tonight, Angie." He said it with all the emotion he was experiencing and gazed deep into her fathomless eyes.

Her smile revealed the happiness his words produced. "Thank you, Simon."

They should have been able to enjoy the dance, but they didn't. Instead they both were anticipating the confrontation that awaited them at the country club. Simon's mother hadn't disappointed him.

"Mom," he said, tucking his arm around Angie's waist. "This is Angela Robinson."

"Hello, Angela." Politely Mrs. Canfield shook Angie's hand, but her eyes had turned questioningly to her son. His mother was far too refined to say anything at the moment, but Simon knew he'd hear about his choice of a date later.

Simon escorted Angie to a dinner table in the front of the room where they were joined by Cal Spencer and his date. No sooner were they seated when Simon's father approached the table, expecting an introduction. He asked the group to excuse Simon and took him across the room, where he proceeded to demand to know exactly what kind of game his son was playing.

"Trouble?" Cal asked when Simon returned.

"No." Simon reached for Angie's hand under the table. "Everything's fine." Only it hadn't been and they both knew it.

Some time later, when Simon was away from the table exchanging polite inanities with a friend of the family, Cal came for him.

"Angie's left."

Simon looked around him in disbelief. "What happened?"

"Someone came up and said her kind wasn't welcome here."

Anger filled every fiber of his being. "Who?" He was ready to swing on the bastard.

"It doesn't matter, does it?" Cal murmured. "Shouldn't you be more concerned about Angie?"

It amazed him how far she'd gotten in so short a time. "Angie," Simon called, running after her. A hand on her shoulder stopped her progress down the hill. Her dark lashes were wet and he knew she'd been crying.

"Oh, Angie." He pulled her into his embrace and wrapped his arms around her. She sniffled once and broke free, pausing to wipe her cheek, but kept her face lowered, refusing to meet his gaze.

"I'm sorry, running away was a childish thing to do, but I couldn't stay there another minute with everyone looking at me and whispering." Her voice was so muted he could hardly hear her.

"Angie, it was my fault." He brought her back into his arms and breathed against her hair, taking in the fresh fragrance. "I should be the one to apologize."

"No." She kept her head down. "I don't think we should see each other again."

Simon was utterly stunned. "You don't mean that."

She shook her head. "We'll talk about it later."

"No, we won't." He held her at arm's length, a

hand on each shoulder. "We'll talk about it now. I love you, Angie Robinson. Do you understand me?"

"Oh, Simon, please don't say that."

"I love you," he repeated.

"Don't, Simon, this isn't funny."

"I tell a girl how I feel and she accuses me of joking? You have a lot to learn about me."

She sniffled and wiped the tears from her face. "Stop it, right now, you hear?"

"I love Angie," he shouted, tossing back his head. He wanted the world to know. Loving Angie wasn't an embarrassment; she was the best thing that had ever happened in his life.

"Simon."

"I love you," he whispered, drawing her into his arms.

"I won't go back there," she whispered defiantly.

"Don't worry, I wouldn't put you through that." With their fingers entwined they walked to the parking lot. From there they drove to their favorite drive-in and ate thick hamburgers.

That summer Angie had gotten a part-time job working at Garland Pharmacy. Simon picked her up in the morning and dropped her back home when she was finished. He sometimes worked at the bank, but he didn't recall that he did much of anything worthwhile.

"Are you going to be working there after college?" Angie asked one night. They were parked in their favorite spot at Three Tree Point.

"I'll probably take over for my dad someday," Simon answered, more interested in kissing Angie's earlobe than talking.

"Is that what you want to do?"

Simon grinned and straightened. Angie had a way of doing this whenever their kissing became too hot and heavy. With any other girl he would have pressed her, but not Angie. He didn't want to do anything she wasn't ready to try. It wasn't easy not to touch her. Some nights he thought the frustration would kill him.

"I've never thought about doing anything else but working in the bank. Why?"

"No reason."

She was quiet after that and didn't resist when he turned her lips to his and kissed her long and hard, pulling her lower lip between his teeth and sucking on it. Angie had a beautiful mouth: wide, soft, passionate. Simon loved the feel of it under his own. But then he loved everything about her.

As usual he dropped her off a block before Oak. She sat for a moment staring at her hands. "Lloyd Sipe was in Garland's today."

"And?"

"He asked me to a movie this weekend."

Simon felt a lead balloon sink in his stomach. "You're not going, are you?"

"I told him I wouldn't."

Simon relaxed.

"But I think it might be a good idea if we didn't see so much of each other for a while."

"Why?" he exploded.

"I'm afraid," she whispered. "Afraid because I love you so much. I . . . I want us both to start seeing others. Just until school starts. We can talk about things in September."

Simon's immediate reaction had been to argue, but eventually she had worn him down. They stopped dating. The separation nearly drove Simon crazy. He loved her, it was only natural that he wanted to be with Angie. But in the months that they'd been seeing each other, something else, something more far-reaching had happened. Angie had become his best friend. Nothing seemed right without her. His life had been ripped open, leaving a gaping hole exposed. Even Cal, who had been Simon's friend since grade school, couldn't fill the gap. For a long time Simon didn't date. He couldn't see that it would do any good. When Angie realized he wasn't seeing other girls, she started dating Lloyd Sipe. Simon got the message and asked out Kate Holston. He found her even more boring than Shirley. Later that summer his mother arranged a date for him with the visiting niece of one of her Garden Club friends. Jill Something-or-other had hidden a pint of vodka in her purse and proceeded to get smashed. By the end of the evening, Simon couldn't drive her back to Auntie fast enough. Laughing, her hair in a wild disarray, Jill had placed her hand high on his thigh and claimed she wasn't in any hurry to get home. If he knew "someplace private" there were lots of things she could think of to do to kill time.

The first day of their senior year, Simon had stopped Angie in the hall. "You said we'd talk. Are you ready?"

She smiled and nodded.

They met outside the library and drove to Three Tree Point. Simon parked the car, turned off the engine and reached for Angie. He held her so hard that for a moment he feared he might have hurt her. "It's not the same," he whispered into her hair. "It'll never be right unless it's you in my arms."

Her own words were muffled as she buried her face in his shoulder, but the strength of her hold told him everything he needed to know.

With Angie, Simon was on the same intellectual and spiritual plane. By early the next spring they were a hairsbreadth from exploring the sexual plane.

"Angie, I love you, I want to marry you."

"Don't ask me," she pleaded, spreading eager kisses across his face. "Please don't ask."

Simon was so inflamed that controlling himself took a superhuman effort. "We've got to stop, Angie. Right now. Do you understand?" He pulled his hand from the full swell of her breasts, to her ribs and finally, when he could control himself, from beneath her cotton sweater.

"Yes," she repeated, her voice soft and willing. "I understand."

He leaned his head against the back of the car seat and took in deep, agonizing breaths.

"Can . . . can you hold me, Simon?" she pleaded. "Just for a few minutes."

"Oh, Angie. This does it," he muttered. "I'm talking to my dad tomorrow."

Angie turned stricken eyes to him. "About what?"

"Us."

"Simon, they're not going to let us get married."

"They can't stop us. I love you. After last summer I know I don't ever want to be without you again."

The confrontation with his parents had been the worst thing Simon had ever faced. Angie had wanted to go with him. Later he thanked God that he hadn't let her. The first thing his mother asked him after he announced that he wanted to marry Angie was if she was pregnant.

Simon couldn't believe that his mother would even suggest such a thing. It only proved that Georgia Canfield didn't know Angie.

"Of course she isn't. We haven't even made love. Angie doesn't want to until we're married."

"Can't you see what she's after?" his father had demanded. "This little girl from Oak Street isn't stupid. Of course she doesn't want to do 'it' until after you're married. Men don't like to pay for what they can get free."

It took all of Simon's restraint not to shout at his parents that it wasn't like that with him and Angie. The taste of gall filled his mouth at the thought that the two people who supposedly loved him so much would try to take the beautiful relationship he shared with Angie and make it into a sordid, ugly thing.

"You're only seventeen," his mother pleaded.

"And in this state you need our permission to marry," Simon, Senior interjected. "And as far as I'm concerned you don't have it."

His father had come to Simon's bedroom later and sat on the mattress beside him. He draped a fatherly arm over his shoulder and assured him that Angie was the type of girl for Simon to sow his wild oats with. No need to marry her kind. Later, he suggested, another girl would come along from the right kind of people, and Simon would feel just as strongly about her. At seventeen, Simon wasn't ready for the responsibilities a wife and possible family would entail. He should have fun with Angie, but be careful that she didn't get pregnant. Simon's jaw had been clenched so tight that his teeth ached for hours afterward.

"You don't need to tell me what they said," Angie murmured when they met later.

"Listen," Simon argued, "I've got everything worked out. We'll get married in September after my birthday."

"But you'll have left for college and . . ."

"I'm not going to the U."

"Simon, you've got to. Your father went there and his father before him."

"Marrying you is more important than some stupid tradition."

Angie's shoulders had drooped as she slowly, sadly, shook her head. "I won't let you do that."

"We don't have any choice."

"Your schooling is important."

"You're the most important thing in my life, Angie."

It had seemed crazy that the only serious rift in their relationship had been over getting married. Angie was adamant that Simon continue with his schooling in the fall. She wouldn't marry him otherwise. What she didn't know was that his father had already anticipated his son's defiance and had threatened to cut off Simon's allowance. Simon could never manage school while making a home for himself and Angie at the same time. As for college, he didn't give a damn. Even when approached about a possible basketball scholarship Simon didn't care. All he cared about was Angie.

Not finding a happy solution to their dilemma, Simon had come up with a compromise. It wasn't the perfect answer. But when he said his vows in the church that night, he had meant every word.

Sweat poured off Simon from his long run just as effortlessly as the memories of Angie had filled his mind. He moved from the long drive-way into the house and headed for the bathroom to shower. Stripping, he turned on the pulsating power spray and turned his face into the jet stream, letting water wash down on him. Even the pounding water whispered Angie's name. He felt like singing. The realization produced a smile. It had been years since he'd sung in the shower.

Stepping onto the bathmat Simon reached for a thick towel. A frown drove his dark brows together. His wet hair glistened as he eased his long arms into the starched dress shirt and fastened the top button. At seventeen he'd been more in love than at any other time in his life, he mused. A love that pure and good wasn't supposed to happen to a rosy-cheeked kid. Most people search a lifetime and never experience what he had those years with Angie. With a vengeance, he jammed the gold cuff link into place.

Dressed now, and ready for the office, Simon poured a cup of hot coffee and glanced at his gold wristwatch. A thousand times he had questioned what a seventeen-year-old boy could know of love. Little, he admitted freely now, but enough to realize that if it wasn't Angie in his arms, it wasn't love. He emptied the coffee cup in the sink and moved to the garage. The turquoise convertible seemed to smile at him. This weekend he'd see about starting her up again. For now he had to hurry or he would be late at the bank.

He parked in his usual spot and jingled the car keys before putting them in his pocket.

Once inside the bank he began whistling as he walked across the large marble floor, drawing his secretary's blank stare.

"Good morning, Mr. Canfield."

"Morning, Mrs. Wilson," he repeated cheerfully. Five people in the bank gaped in surprise.

His secretary took twenty minutes to locate Angie's business number in Charleston. Simon had lost her once, he wasn't going to make that mistake again. He loved Angie as much now as he had twelve years ago.

His heart was pounding as he punched in the telephone number. She answered on the third ring.

Five

The sharp corners of Angie's mind were crowded with a thousand niggling thoughts. She should be thinking of Glenn, not Simon. She was home now and engaged to a wonderful man who loved her. And she loved Glenn in return, only . . . only things in Groves Point hadn't turned out as she'd expected. She had hoped to find Simon married and happy with a house full of rambunctious children. Instead she'd found a bitter, disillusioned man trapped in the limbo that had held her prisoner all these years. She had traveled to Groves Point seeking release from the past. The trip had given her that and washed away the guilt that had plagued her from the moment she had accepted the money from Georgia Canfield. But with the release came another set of regrets. Simon.

Determinedly she pushed thoughts of him to the back of her mind and zipped up the soft pink smock that hung from a hook in the back of her shop, Clay Pots. It had been named for her father, and he was proud of her small business venture. She hadn't told Clay about her weekend trip. It was better that he never know. Her father had yet to learn that she had accepted Glenn's proposal. The three of them were having dinner together

Thursday night. Glenn and Angie planned to tell Clay then. Not that he'd be surprised.

"Morning, Donna."

"Morning." Donna was busy placing the cut flowers in the refrigerated compartment in the front of the shop and didn't glance up.

Angie's one full-time employee worked the early shift and stopped on her way in to the shop to buy cut flowers direct from the wholesaler.

"Angie." Donna stuck her blond head around the glass case. "There was a phone call for you earlier. I left the name on your desk."

"Thanks." Absently, Angie leafed through the orders for the day, dividing them between Donna and herself. Donna manned the counter in the morning and Angie took over in the afternoon.

Her heartbeat came to an abrupt halt when she glanced at the pink slip on her desk. The note was brief: Simon Canfield phoned, will try again later.

Every time the phone rang for the next four hours, Angie stiffened and prayed it wasn't Simon. Everything had already been said. All Angie wanted to do was bury the hurts of the past and build a new life from the ashes of Groves Point. She couldn't think of what to say to Simon or how to explain to him her unreasonable feelings. It would sound ridiculous to shout at him that it wasn't supposed to have happened this way. Erroneously, she had assumed him to be married and happy. She wanted to tuck him neatly

98

into a private corner of her life, like a favorite book once treasured, but now outgrown.

"You're as jumpy as a bullfrog today," Donna complained early in the afternoon. "What's the matter with you?"

"Nothing," she lied. As she spoke the phone pealed. Something inside her, an innate alarm system, warned her even before she picked up the receiver that it was Simon.

"Clay Pots."

Simon chuckled. "Now where did you ever come up with a name like that?"

"Hello, Simon." She knew she sounded stiff and unnatural, but she couldn't help it. She realized that turning her back to Donna would only arouse her employee's suspicions. Her hand tightened around the receiver until the pressure pinched her ear.

"Hello, Angie. Is this a busy time? Should I phone back later?"

Briefly, she toyed with the idea of delaying this conversation. Even a few hours would help her compose her thoughts.

"Angie?"

"No . . . no, this is as good a time as any."

"I want to see you. I haven't stopped thinking about you since you left. There's so much we left unsaid, and more that needs to be made right."

Angie closed her eyes and measured her words

carefully. "Simon, listen to me. What happened is in the past. We can't resurrect that now."

"Why not?" he argued. "I love you."

"You love a memory. I'm not a sweet, naive teenager anymore. I can't go back to being seventeen."

"Me neither, but I'm anxious to meet the woman you've become." His voice went low and seductive, as if he'd put his hand over the mouthpiece so not to be overheard. "I'm eager to show you the man I am now."

Angie's heart slammed to her knees. Her throat went dry and she discovered she couldn't speak.

The bell over the door chimed, indicating that someone had entered the shop. Angie was so grateful she could have cried. "I've got to go, a customer just came in."

"Angie, listen, I'll phone you later."

"Simon, don't. Please, don't." Angry with herself for being so weak, she didn't wait for his farewell, and replaced the receiver. With a forced smile, she turned toward the delivery man who was approaching the counter.

Simon stared at the auditor's report on his desk, knowing he couldn't concentrate on it when thoughts of Angie dominated his mind. His phone conversation with her earlier had been awkward. Damn, he should be in Charleston, not Groves Point. He needed to talk to her face-to-face and not try to carry on a serious conversation with customers walking in and out of her shop every few minutes. But with his father away from the bank so much of the time now, Simon couldn't pick up and leave. He rubbed a hand across his eyes to ease the growing pain that throbbed at his temple. The walls seemed to close in around him and he stood, jerking his suit coat from the back of his chair.

"Mrs. Wilson, I'll be back in an hour," he announced to his secretary on his way out the door.

"But Mr. C-Canfield . . ." she stuttered. "What should I do about your two o'clock appointment?"

Irritation furrowed his brows. "Reschedule it," he snapped, then stalked from the room before she could comment further.

Georgia Canfield was in the backyard, pruning her rosebushes. A straw hat graced her silver head and was secured under her chin by a brightly colored scarf. Spotless white gloves hid her veined hands. At a glance, his mother looked like an aged Southern belle of the era of the War between the States.

"Hello, Mother."

"Simon." She spoke without turning. "I wondered how long it would take you to come."

"Then you know why."

Turning, she set the wicker basket filled with

blossoms on the wrought-iron table. "Sit down and I'll ring for coffee."

Without question, Simon did as requested. The urge to hurl accusations at his mother seared his mind, and he clenched his fists with burning irritation.

The maid quietly delivered a tray with two cups of coffee. Resolutely, Simon glanced away, counting the interminable seconds before he could speak. At the sound of the retreating steps, he returned his attention to his mother. She sat across from him at the round ornate table.

"I understand that Angela returned the money," Georgia Canfield began without preamble. She offered no excuse or explanation, but added two lumps of sugar to her coffee and stirred it briskly. From her outward appearance they could have been discussing the unusually mild weather instead of the gross interference in his life.

Not for the first time, Simon marveled at his mother's aplomb. Sometimes the sheer bravado of her actions astonished him. From his youth, Simon had been taught to look upon his mother as fragile and delicate. At all costs she was to be protected from the cruelties of life. Now he felt as if he needed protection from her.

"Is that all you have to say?" he demanded in starched tones.

"I did what I thought was best."

"You interfered in my life."

A nerve near Georgia's eye twitched, and she set the china cup in the saucer. "Don't raise your voice to me, Simon."

It took everything in him not to cry out at the injustice of her actions. The hurt and betrayal must have shone in his eyes.

"I don't expect you to understand why I acted as I did, nor do I expect your approval," Georgia continued calmly.

Unable to sit politely in the chair, Simon vaulted to his feet. "If you think I've come to applaud your wisdom, Mother, you're wrong."

"No," she replied evenly, "I don't imagine you did."

"And what did Dad have to say about this?" Simon doubted his father's involvement. Not that he was incapable of this deception, only that ten thousand sounded like far more than Simon, Senior would have parted with freely.

The slim hand shook perceptively as she sipped from the edge of the dainty cup. "He was in full agreement. Something had to be done. You were barely eighteen and on the brink of your college career. Angela Robinson was ruining that."

"I was in love."

"You were too young to know about love."

"And when I married Carol I was mature enough to know that kind of thing. Is that what you're saying?"

"At twenty-one, I would say so. Yes, you were."

"Do you want the real reason my marriage failed, Mother? The honest to God reason?"

"Simon, please, that was all a long time ago. Let's not drag up this unpleasantness."

"You handpicked Carol yourself, but you made one basic mistake, Mother dear. I was still in love with Angie. I married another woman because I'd given up the hope that Angie would ever come back. I didn't love Carol then, and God forgive me, I didn't love her the whole miserable year we were together."

Georgia Canfield went as pale as alabaster. No longer did she make the pretense of sipping her afternoon coffee. Her eyes became dull and lifeless. Simon's divorce had devastated his mother. Carol had become the daughter Georgia had never had, the one woman Georgia could mold into a replica of herself. The two had taken delight in the pointless avocations that filled his mother's life: bridge, the Garden Club and numerous charities. For months following Carol and Simon's separation and divorce his mother had held the hope that they would get back together. Not until Carol remarried did Georgia abandon the possibility of a reconciliation.

For Simon it had been only when Carol remarried that he was released from the guilt of having married a woman he didn't love.

Pulling the long white envelope from inside his jacket, Simon placed it on the table in front of his mother. "Unfortunately, the cost of sending Angie away was higher than you assumed."

"Simon?" A faint pleading quality entered her voice.

"Angie's repaid that now, but I doubt that you'll ever regain my respect."

Painfully, Georgia Canfield lowered her gaze to the envelope, knowing its contents without being told. "I'll ask only one thing of you, Simon. Your father's health isn't good. Don't mention this to him." She hesitated and added softly, "Please."

The air conditioner kicked on, and soothing cool air drifted into Angie's small apartment, relieving the intense afternoon heat. Barefoot, her hair swept up on her head, she filled the claw-footed cast-iron tub with water. Now that the money had been repaid, she could think about moving to a more modern apartment. The thought caused her to pause. No. Soon she'd be married to Glenn and they'd find a nice place to live. It bothered Angie the way Glenn escaped her mind. She did love him, she rationalized, she was confused right now, that was all.

The tub was filled, and still Angie stood with her cotton bathrobe loosely tied at her waist. The urge to locate her high-school annual from her senior year drove her to the bedroom. She crouched down on her knees, and dragged out the narrow flat box from under her bed. Sitting cross-legged

105

on the polished hardwood floor, she lifted off the cardboard lid. Memories sprang out and danced around her at all sides. On the top, in a sealed bag, was the crushed corsage that Simon had given her for the junior-senior prom when they were sixteen. Those were the first flowers any boy had ever given her, and Angie had treasured them more than riches. Even when Georgia Canfield had sent Angie away, she hadn't been able to part with these memories. Reverently she set the corsage aside and pulled out the yearbook she sought. With a sense of unreality she turned the pages and stared at the picture of herself as valedictorian of the graduating class. Had she really ever been that young and innocent? A sad smile touched her eyes. For someone so intelligent, she had been incredibly stupid.

She turned the pages one by one and a slow smile grew until it hovered on the verge of laughter. She wasn't the only one who looked young and innocent. Bob and Cindy were barely recognizable. And Simon, the gray eyes that stared back at her were so serious; his dark hair was several inches longer than the way it was currently styled. They'd changed, all of them. Without conscious effort, Angie realized that her index finger was brushing over the black-and-white photo of Simon.

The doorbell chimed and shook her from the deep retrospection. A moment passed before she realized what was causing the noise. Stumbling to her feet she tightened the sash of the thin housecoat and hurried into the living room. A glance through the peephole confirmed her visitor was Glenn.

Angie unlocked the dead bolt and pulled open the door. "Glenn, I apologize, I'm running a little behind schedule tonight."

His loving smile was filled with a warmth women dream of seeing in a man. "I don't mind," he said, taking her in his arms. His mouth claimed hers, parting her lips in a deep, languorous kiss. Angie linked her arms around his neck and tried to kiss him back and found she couldn't. *You'll learn,* her mind assured her, and Angie didn't doubt that she would.

Glenn's grip relaxed and his hand continued to hold her loosely. "I've had quite a day," he announced and kissed the tip of her nose. "I'm finding that I like being engaged, but I have a feeling I'm going to like marriage a whole lot more."

Tipping her head back, Angie smiled into his shining eyes. "I'm sure I am, too." This man loved her, and she wasn't going to let anything ruin that. "Pour yourself a drink while I hop in the tub."

"Are you sure you don't want company?"

Angie's laugh was light and breezy. "I don't know. That sounds interesting."

She'd been teasing and was surprised when Glenn followed her into the bedroom. He stopped short at the papers, books and pressed flowers scattered about the floor.

"What's this?"

Instinctively, Angie bit into her bottom lip. She'd rather not explain, but Glenn had a right to know. "I was looking through some things I saved from high school."

"In Groves Point?" His eyes met hers in a sober exchange.

Angie nodded, sitting on the edge of the mattress. "I can't believe I was ever that young."

Glenn bent down and retrieved the annual that lay open on the floor. Sitting on the bed beside her, he turned the pages to the senior pictures and grinned when he found hers.

"You go ahead and look while I take a bath," she suggested with feigned disinterest. Her back was to him as she took a sleeveless summer dress from the closet.

"Is there anyone else's picture I should look for?" Glenn asked in a bland voice that revealed all.

A tingling sensation ran up her spine, and Angie's fingers groped and bit into the wire hanger. Removing the dress gave her vital seconds to collect her thoughts. She was marrying Glenn, he had a right to know. "Simon Canfield's."

"And he is?"

"Was," Angie corrected. "Simon was the first man I loved."

"Heart and soul?"

"And body." Angie didn't leave room for any misunderstanding.

A heavy silence fell over the room. When Glenn made no response, Angie turned, her gaze seeking his. For months Glenn had lovingly wooed her. He had courted her in word and deed in the most romantic of ways. Eventually his persistence had won her over enough to encourage her to face the past head-on.

Sending her back to Groves Point had been a measure of how much he did love her. The hurt in his eyes now revealed the pain her words had caused him. Angie could offer no vindications or apologies. Nor could she alter the circumstances of years long past.

Saddened, her eyes glistened with unshed tears of regret. The last person she ever wanted to hurt was Glenn. He was the only man patient enough to peel down the barriers she had erected about herself.

Closing the book, he set it aside. "He was the one you went to see in Groves Point."

"Yes."

Their eyes were level now, unflinching. A minute passed before he spoke. "Go ahead and take your bath and I'll get myself that drink."

The questions in Glenn's eyes were shouting at her, demanding some kind of explanation. But he asked for none. The tension flowed from Angie until her knees felt weak with relief.

The bath water was lukewarm by the time she had settled in the bubbly surface and washed. Her mind was crowded, uneasy. She had agreed to be Glenn's wife. Maintaining secrets, even the most painful ones, was not the way to start their lives together. Before her resolve could weaken, Angie stood and roughly dried herself with a bath towel, rubbing her sensitive skin with unnecessary force. Hurriedly she dressed and moved into the living room.

Glenn was standing with his back to her, staring out the window to the parking lot below.

"Glenn."

"Angie."

They both spoke at once, then laughed nervously.

"You go first." He took a sip of the bourbon as if to brace himself, his dark eyes uncertain. Glenn was such a positive, forthright man that it was a shock to read the wavering doubts in him. He loved her, and dear God, she didn't want to hurt him.

"You should know . . ." she began, then paused and gestured weakly with her hands. "The thing is, I don't know where to start."

"Will one of these help?" He held up his drink

and the chunks of ice clinked against the rim.

"I think it would."

Angie so rarely drank anything stronger than wine that when she took a sip, the burning feeling sank to the pit of her stomach and stayed there like a red-hot coal. Grimacing, she handed the glass back to Glenn. "I'll do better without this."

"From the look about you, I think I may need it." With a tumbler in each hand he sat across from her, resting his elbows on bent knees. White lines of tension bracketed his mouth. Playfully, he took a sip from each drink and found her eyes. "Go on, I'm ready now."

Angie knew what it had cost him to make light of this situation and appreciated him all the more. "I don't deserve you, Glenn."

"Just don't tell me you're married and have five kids waiting for you in Groves Point."

Her pain-shadowed eyes dropped to her hands. "There were no children," she whispered brokenly.

"But you were married?"

"Yes . . . no." This was the worst part. How could she possibly explain that through all these years she *felt* married?

"Which is it?"

"I was married to Simon, but the marriage wasn't legal."

"You'd better start at the beginning," he murmured after a lengthy pause, his voice aching and confused.

They talked nonstop for an hour until there was nothing Glenn didn't understand or know. When Angie was only a few minutes into the painful details, Glenn crossed the room and sat beside her, holding her close, lending her his strength. Angie was amazed that she could recount the events with such a lack of emotion. It was almost as if she were relating another person's story. Angie started the story when Simon and she were in high school, and ended with the bitter man she had found in Groves Point Citizens Federal and her confrontation with his mother the following evening. Sparing no particulars, accusing no one, she completed her narration and paused to study the grave look on Glenn's face.

"If you have any questions, ask them now," she requested softly, surprised at the dry, parched feeling in her throat. "After tonight, I want us to make a pact to never speak of Simon or Groves Point again."

Glenn was motionless beside her. "I don't think that will work," he said finally.

"Why not?"

"Because if I were Simon I'd be here right now. From everything you've said about him, I'm surprised he hasn't arrived already."

"Why?" Angie asked, unsure. She wanted to bury the past, not resurrect it. "No, he won't," she returned, sounding more confident than she felt. "I told him it's over and that he's dredging up a memory. I asked him not to phone again."

Angie felt the room temperature drop ten degrees. "He phoned?"

"Today . . . I told him it's over. We can't go back to being seventeen again."

"Is it really over, Angie?"

"Yes," she cried, her mind in turmoil. "Would I have agreed to be your wife otherwise?"

Naked uncertainty flashed across his handsome face as he clasped her hands tightly within his own. "I want to believe that."

"Oh, Glenn. My first instinct is to suggest that we go away and get married tonight. That would settle everything. But I can't. And I won't."

"I wouldn't do that." Glenn drew in a long labored breath. "Everything will be right for us and between us when I make you my wife." His voice was soft with tenderness.

Angie turned brilliant eyes to him and smiled her thanksgiving. He was telling her that he understood her need to do everything properly this time. Her marriage to him wasn't going to be a hushed affair, with their vows whispered behind closed doors in the dead of night. She wanted to stand before God and friends and proclaim their love. With Glenn she would have a maid-of-honor and bridesmaids and her picture in the paper. This marriage was for a lifetime and there would be nothing to make it sordid. In the years to come she would look back and remember the joy in Glenn's eyes when he slipped the wedding band on her finger. This marriage would be a good one, and with it would come the years of happiness that had been so elusive for the past twelve years. The pain in her heart that had spread like cancer into every facet of her life would forever be healed.

Threading his fingers through her hair, he framed her oval face between his hands and gazed into her eyes. "I love you, Angie."

With a sublime effort, Angie forced herself to smile and echo his words.

"The same man as yesterday called," Donna announced when Angie entered the back door of the flower shop the next morning.

Angie dragged her gaze from her friend to the desk and the offending telephone. "Did he leave a message?"

"No. Only that he'd phone back later."

Angie panicked, then became ice-cold as resentment filled every pore of her body. "If he phones again, tell him I'm not here. Better yet, inform him I've taken a six-month cruise to Antarctica."

Donna stared at her with wide-eyed astonishment. Angie instantly regretted her outburst, ashamed that she was crumbling because Simon Canfield had tried to contact her for the second time in two days.

The worst part, she thought, was that she couldn't chastise and berate him for interfering in her life. They shared a special bond of friendship, love, marriage and betrayal. Simon could never be just an old "boyfriend" in her life, and finding the proper place in which to fit him could be impossible.

Angie's eyes strayed back to the phone. She hardly believed the surge of emotion she was experiencing. Vividly she recalled the look in Simon's eyes as she had pulled out of the gravel driveway on his property. His gray eyes had grown soft with confusion as if he wasn't sure if he should let her go or plead with her to stay.

The phone rang again ten minutes later. Donna's eye sought hers. "Do you want me to get it?"

"No." She shook her head as she spoke. "I will."

She drew in her breath and squared her shoulders as she walked to her desk in the rear of the shop. The area was small but granted her more privacy than if she were standing at the front counter.

"Clay Pots."

"Angie, it's Simon."

His voice was a gentle caress filled with the tenderness she had known from him in her youth. A surge of unexpected compassion spread over her, warming her. "Simon, before you say anything there's something you should know. Something important."

"Nothing could be more important than the fact I love you, Angie Robinson. Listen, I'm doing everything I can to make arrangements to—"

"Simon, please, will you listen to me?"

"Good. We need to talk. There are a few too many skeletons in our closets."

"I can't talk now," she insisted. "Not in the middle of the day."

"It's not even nine."

"That's the middle of the day to a florist. Are you going to spend good money arguing with me long distance?" She nearly choked at how ridiculous that must have sounded. Simon Canfield drove a forty-thousand-dollar car, lived on choice South Carolina soil and dressed in five-hundred-dollar suits. Prime-time rates on a long-distance phone call weren't even worthy of a mention.

"I want to see you."

"No." It took all her restraint not to cry at him to stop pressuring her like this.

"Why not?"

Tell him you're engaged, her mind screamed. *He's got to know. It's the only thing that will get through to him now.* "I won't see you, it's too painful."

"Angie, I swear to you, I'll never hurt you again."

116

"Oh, Simon." Her voice became a throbbing whisper. "There's something you've got to know."

"Angie, please listen to me—"

"No," she cried shakily. Her hand pressed against her forehead and lifted the hair from her brow. "There's someone else who loves me now. He's a good man—I know you'd like him." Her voice cracked, and she sucked in a calming breath.

A stunned silence echoed over the line.

"Please, Simon, don't phone me again," she begged. "I don't want to hurt you. Just leave me alone." Blind determination gave her the courage to sever the connection. Her hand remained on the phone, half expecting Simon to immediately call again. Hundreds of miles might be separating them, but it didn't take much to imagine the cold displeasure hardening Simon's face. Simon was a man who was accustomed to getting what he wanted. A full five minutes passed before she gave up the vigil. And it was another couple of minutes more before she realized that Donna was regarding her with a worried frown.

In a flower shop the phone was essential to run a profitable business. Angie learned that day to hate it. With every ring she cringed, fearing it was Simon. No day had ever lasted so long. She was out the door at ten minutes after five, relieved to have escaped partially unscathed.

This was the night she and Glenn were having dinner with her father. An evening to celebrate. Glenn was bringing his grandmother's ring to her and they were going to announce their engagement.

"This should be the happiest day in your life," Angie muttered out loud as she slipped her feet into delicate high-heeled sandals. "At least try to look the part." She checked her appearance in the mirror and groaned. Clay would take one look at her and demand to know who died.

"Damn," she groaned and pinched her cheeks, hoping that at least would add color to her ashen features.

As usual Glenn was on time. His mouth caressed hers in a slow, undemanding kiss. "Are you feeling okay?"

Nodding took a monumental effort. "I'm fine."

The doorbell chimed in short, impatient bursts, and Angie tossed a stricken glance across the room. Panic filled her and her gaze flew to Glenn.

"Do you want me to get it?" he asked, almost tenderly.

"Please." Apprehension rooted her to the floor.

Glenn walked across the room and pulled open the door. "Hello, Simon," he said firmly. "I've been expecting you. I'm Angie's fiancé."

≈ Six ≈

Charleston had often been called the Holy City. Her skyline punctuated with the graceful spires of churches, the symbols of man's faith in a merciful God. Angie's faith was at its lowest ebb as she sat beside Glenn in his Oldsmobile. Silently, he drove to the elegant Philippe Million restaurant where her father was meeting them for dinner.

Angie's thoughts drifted to the scene they had recently endured. Simon and Glenn had faced each other like warlords defending their titles. At Glenn's announcement that he and Angie were engaged, Simon had turned his disbelieving gaze to her, demanding that she tell him it wasn't true. Instead, Angie had inched closer to Glenn's side. To her surprise, Glenn didn't place a proprietary arm around her.

"Does he know about us?" Simon directed his question to Angie, ignoring Glenn.

"Everything," Angie told him.

Simon continued to concentrate his fierce gaze on her. "We need to talk."

"As you can see, Angie and I are going out tonight," Glenn intervened, continuing to shock Angie even more.

Her thoughts drifted to the present as Glenn pulled to a stop at a red light and turned to her, laying his hand over hers. "Are you angry?" He looked as if he could stand fearless against the strongest enemy, but crumble under her distrust.

"Angry?" she echoed, and her graceful features scowled. "How can I be? Why, oh, why, do you have to be so noble? I don't want to see Simon again. I honestly want him out of my life."

Glenn's face tightened as he returned his attention to the road. "As much as I love you, as much as I want you to be my wife, I can't see us ever truly happy with the shadow of Simon looming between us."

"I went back to Groves Point," she argued. Already she had done everything he'd asked of her. More. The future stretched before her like an eagerly awaited journey, and for the first time this heavy load of guilt and unhappiness had been lifted. She was free. It wasn't right that Glenn was forcing her to turn around and go back.

A weary smile briefly relaxed the tight lines about his mouth. "Yes, my love, but you didn't bury the past, you simply stirred it up."

Smoothing an imaginary wrinkle from her favorite blue skirt, Angie spoke again. "But I don't want to see Simon." If Glenn harbored small doubts, then hers were giant mountains.

Glenn's hand reached for hers and squeezed it lightly, lending her his conviction. "He's only here for a few days. If you don't spend time with him then you'll always wonder. We both will."

Again Angie marveled at this man beside her. He loved her enough to risk losing her. And although he presented a facade of unwavering confidence, Angie recognized that he wasn't entirely convinced things would work out as he desired. "I don't want anything more than to be your wife," she said.

"Good."

The restaurant came into view, presenting another complication. "Glenn," she breathed, "what are we going to tell Clay?"

"Nothing."

"But . . ."

"My grandmother's diamond is in my pocket, but as much as I want to slip that ring on your finger, I won't. The time isn't right for you to wear it now. Spend this weekend with Simon. A few days will make all the difference in the world."

That was exactly what Angie feared the most. Another concern bobbed to the surface of her mind. Her father. "Clay mustn't know I was in Groves Point."

They exchanged meaningful glances. "Is it the money?"

"Yes."

"Whatever happened to it?"

She lifted one delicate shoulder, not wanting to say the words.

"Clay spent it?"

"It gave him the chance to follow his dreams. He's a wonderful musician," she said a trifle too defiantly. "He went to Nashville looking for a chance to sell his songs."

"And blew it." Glenn completed the sad tale in three simple words.

"I don't think he's ever forgiven himself. Although he never mentions the Canfields he hates them almost as much as he detests Groves Point."

Clay had followed his dreams and in doing so had shattered Angie's. With the money in his hands, he had become a stranger. He left Angie staggering with shock and grief in Charleston and bought a souped-up jalopy to drive to Nashville. The way to impress the powers-that-be was with money, Clay had claimed. He'd return, he promised, as rich as Rockefeller. Wealthier than the Canfields, at least. Within a month he was back, broke and broken. For a time he tried to convince Angie that she had sold herself cheap, and that the thing to do was to return to Groves Point and get more money. For the first time in her life, Angie refused her father something. Now he hated Groves Point and the entire population. His music would never be sung, and it was easier to blame the Canfields than to accept fault with his own actions.

"But he's going to wonder why we're celebrating. In all the time we've been going out, we've never taken Dad to a fancy restaurant. He's expecting us to announce our engagement. What are we going to tell him?"

Glenn grinned suddenly. "We'll simply have to make up something. Should I tell him you're pregnant?"

"Glenn!"

"All right, you come up with something."

In the end, they called it a belated Father's Day gift, until a sober, disappointed Clay reminded Angie that she had already given him a shirt and tie.

Friday morning, Angie must have glanced at her wristwatch fifteen times between eleven and eleven-thirty.

"You're doing your bullfrog routine again," Donna mentioned casually. "You sure have been jumpy this week."

Arguing with Donna would be useless, especially since she was right. In spite of herself Angie glanced at her watch again. Simon had said he'd be by to pick her up for lunch between eleven and noon.

The door opened and Angie looked up. Her breath froze in her throat, nearly choking her. Simon's smile was filled with a wealth of love. A slow, admiring grin crept across his features. He was dressed casually in an open-collared sport shirt and cotton slacks. Angie couldn't recall him looking more devastatingly handsome. Her eyes were glued to him, and for the life of her she couldn't speak or move.

Donna's gaze swung from the immobile Angie to Simon and then back to Angie.

"Can I help you?" Donna intervened, obviously confused.

"I've come to take your employer to lunch."

Angie's fingers worked furiously with the satin ribbon she was forming into a huge bow. With a dexterity that came with years of practice, she wove the ribbon in and out of her fingers, twisted it with a thin wire and set it aside for Donna to insert into a floral centerpiece.

"Are you ready?" Simon directed the question to her.

"Yes. Give me a minute."

Donna's face scrunched up with a frown. "You're the man who called earlier this week."

Simon's gaze didn't waver from Angie's. "Yes."

Flustered and eager to make her escape before Donna asked any more questions, Angie moved around to the front of the counter. "I'll be back at two."

"Make it three." Simon's gaze traveled to Donna as he flashed her a quick smile.

Once outside, Angie squinted in the sunlight of early afternoon. Simon strolled at a leisurely pace through the historic section of Charleston.

Actually, Simon strolled and Angie followed, her arms crossed in front of her to convey her feelings about this arrangement. They drifted in and out of quaint shops along the way, browsing. Simon didn't seem to be in a hurry, but Angie had never been more willing to have an afternoon out of the way.

"Are you hungry?" he asked after an hour.

Her stomach was in tight knots. "Not particularly."

"You know, if you don't loosen up a bit someone might mistake you for a wooden Indian."

"Very funny."

Reaching out, Simon pressed a forefinger to the curve of her cheek. "None of this is the least bit amusing. Let's find someplace to sit and talk."

Simon chose the restaurant. Angie was too wrapped up in her feelings to notice the name. The hostess directed them to a table in the sun and handed them large menus. Angie couldn't have choked down soup let alone an entire meal. This meeting was awkward and unpleasant. Yet Simon appeared oblivious to it all. With the least bit of encouragement he looked as though he would pull her into his arms and kiss her senseless. Angie was determined that he wouldn't get that opportunity.

Simon studied the menu without reading a word. This wasn't going well. He had spent the morning finding out everything he could about

Glenn Lambert. The man had a good reputation as a stockbroker and investor and was coming up in the largest brokerage firm in Charleston. More important was the fact that Glenn loved Angie. They both did. Under different circumstances Simon would have liked the man. Lambert was an experienced gambler, but he was a fool to risk losing Angie. Now it was up to Simon to press that to his advantage. Too much was at stake to lose her again.

The waitress arrived, and Simon ordered the special of the day not knowing what it was. Angie ordered the same. Maybe they would both be surprised, he thought.

"When did you cut your hair?" Simon didn't know why he asked that, but anything was better than the tense silence between them.

Angie spread the starched linen napkin across her lap. It gave her something to do with her fingers as she composed her thoughts. She then lifted her gaze, looking directly into Simon's eyes. "A long time ago. I don't remember when."

He acknowledged her answer with a brief nod.

"When did you cut down the tree?" She had neither the time nor the patience to skirt around the issues.

His fingers tightened around the water glass. "Two years ago June seventh."

Their anniversary. In a flash Angie knew. She knew! Her breath jammed in her lungs as the

126

knowledge seared her mind. He'd chopped down the tree because he couldn't endure the agony of having it in the clearing as mute witness to her betrayal.

She dropped her gaze, trying to find the words to comfort him, afraid that if she stated her true feelings it would complicate an already uncomfortable situation.

"I don't think we need worry," she murmured, drawing in a long, quavering breath. "Our divorce wasn't any more legal than our marriage."

A shadow of pain crossed his features. "It's not that simple. I married you with my heart and discovered it was impossible to divorce you."

They each grew silent then, trapped in the muddy undertow of pain-filled memories.

By the time their lunch arrived, Angie's linen napkin was a mass of wrinkles from all the nervous twisting she had done. Simon had depleted his water glass twice.

Simon was annoyed with himself at being so unnerved by this encounter. Angie hadn't left his mind from the moment he had found her in the clearing last weekend. All week he had carried a clear picture of her in his mind. Now they sat like uncomfortable strangers not knowing what to say. It was obvious that she was frightened. For that matter so was he. Dear Lord, he didn't want to lose her. She was everything he had always known she would be: sweet, fresh, vital. He adored her frankness, her spirit, her capacity to love.

"How long have you known Glenn?"

The question came at her from out of the blue, causing the tight line of her mouth to crack with the beginnings of a smile. They had come to bury the past, and Simon was already challenging the present.

"We met two years ago when I invested the capital from the Petal Pusher."

"The what?"

Deliberately, she set the fork down beside the plate. "For three years I had two businesses. Clay Pots and another I called the Petal Pusher."

"Petal Pusher? What was that?"

"I made weekly visits to restaurants, doctors' offices, or anyplace else that needed someone to come in and make sure their plants were healthy. It seems surveys prove that patients who wait in a doctor's office with dead and dying plants sitting in the corner lose confidence in their physicians."

Simon was enthralled. The idea was a marvelous one. "What happened to the business?"

Angie didn't hesitate. "I sold it for seven thousand dollars profit, invested that until I had the ten I owed you, plus the necessary interest."

"And that's how you met Glenn."

"Right."

"You always were the clever one," Simon said and a thread of pride laced his words.

For the first time that afternoon, Angie lowered her defenses. "I prefer to be thought of as intelligent. I simply found a need and filled it."

"Do you still play tennis?"

Simon had taught her the strenuous game and lived to regret it. Less than six months after he demonstrated the proper method of holding the racket, she was beating him at his own game. "Twice a week. What about you?"

"I've switched to racquetball. If you like I'll teach you that, too."

Glenn already had, but Angie preferred tennis. "No, thanks." She made a show of looking at her watch. "I should be getting back. A teenager comes in part-time on Friday afternoons, and Donna likes to leave a little early."

"It's barely two." He studied Angie and made a conscious effort not to argue. "Will you have dinner with me tonight?"

"Simon," Angie groaned. "It isn't going to do any good to continue to see me. We're different people now with nothing in common except a lot of pain. I'd rather we buried it and went on with our lives."

"Fine. I want that, too, but I also want you in my life. Now and forever."

Clenching her fist, Angie deposited her napkin on the table and pushed back her chair to stand.

"Tonight?"

Glenn's words echoed in the chambers of her

mind. Neither of them wanted the shadow of Simon looming between them. "All right," she agreed reluctantly.

That evening, dressed in a short-sleeved Caribbean-blue linen suit, Angie nervously paced the living-room floor. She now regretted having succumbed so easily to Simon's wishes. Tonight was it, she argued silently with herself. She wouldn't see him again. Every meeting was a strain-filled confrontation that left her facing nagging doubts she preferred to ignore. Yes, she agreed, Glenn was right to force her into doing this, but she hated it.

Nervously she glanced at the wall clock. Clay had a habit of sometimes dropping by unannounced on Friday nights. The last thing she needed was to have him find her with Simon Canfield.

She stood by the window of the second-story apartment and gazed to the lot below. From her position, she viewed Simon's Mercedes pull into the parking lot. The vehicle looked incongruous with the cheaper models that filled the spaces. Unfolding his long powerful legs, he climbed from behind the steering wheel, paused and leaned over the retrieve a small box. Even from this distance, Angie recognized what it was. She should, she had seen others like it often enough. Simon, dear, wonderful, Simon, was bringing her a corsage. No one but him would think to do that for someone who owned a flower shop.

Opening the apartment door she stared at him, hardly able to believe what she saw and felt. Simon, who could afford to give her the most expensive orchids, had brought her a corsage of white roses and blue carnations, made in the very shape and color of the one he had given her for the junior-senior prom.

Their eyes met in silent communication as he walked into the apartment.

"Hello, again," he said, handing her the plastic container.

Numb fingers reached for it as unshed tears glistened in her eyes. "Thank you."

"You're most welcome." His look was full of warmth, and he smiled at her with gentle understanding. "A boy remembers things, too."

Her fingers fumbled with the opening as she struggled to avoid his knowing gaze.

"There are a lot of other things I remember, including this." He reached for her and slowly bent his head toward hers. She knew he was going to kiss her, but instead of pushing away, she lifted her face and met him halfway, seeking the proof that she needed. She loved Glenn and what she had shared with Simon was over. His kiss would confirm that.

Simon's mouth caressed hers in a long, tender exploration, and Angie's theory went soaring into space. Deepening the kiss, Simon shaped and molded her lips to his own. Angie realized that with the least resistance he would let her pull away at any time. Part of her was demanding that she do exactly that. Instead, she dropped the corsage and slipped her arms up and over his shoulders, her fingers seeking the patch of hair that grew at his nape.

"Dear Lord, Angie," he groaned, weaving his fingers into the thick length of her hair. His hands cupped her face as he studied the doubtful, almost accusing light in her eyes. His slow, compelling smile was followed with equally unhurried, lingering kisses that caused her world to orbit crazily. His tongue teased her, first outlining the gentle contours of her mouth, urging, then insisting that she part her lips and grant him the entry he requested. Alternately, he tormented and teased her until she was only too happy to oblige him. The second she parted her lips, his tongue plunged into her mouth in a sensuous attack that left her trembling uncontrollably and clinging to him with an unaccustomed helplessness. Fierce, untamed sensation shot through her as he repeated the assault. His hands roamed her back while he intimately explored her mouth. Gradually his reach extended to the undersides of her buttocks and he lifted her, fitting her body to his so that she could feel his rising passion.

Her mouth broke from his. "No more," she pleaded.

In response he groaned and crushed her tightly to the hard length of his body. At the same moment his mouth came down on hers, silencing the forming protest. Trapped in a fever of long-ing, Angie surrendered and tentatively touched her tongue to his.

Simon groaned again, louder, his mouth leaving hers to explore her earlobe before blazing a path across her cheek, then covering her lips again. His hands released her and moved to the front of her, searing her heated flesh with every intimate brushing against the scented hollow of her throat. His fingers slid slowly across her breasts as he began unbuttoning the thin blouse, seeking the fullness of her breasts. His palms covered them, kneading them in slow, lazy caresses until her nipples stood proud and erect, swelling within his hands.

This newest intrusion penetrated Angie's senses and drugged with passion, she battled desperately for reality by jerking free. Immediately, Simon relaxed his hold and Angie went stumbling back-ward.

Expertly, Simon caught her in his arms and hauled her back into his embrace. "Okay, love, we'll stop." His voice was little more than a throbbing whisper, as he rubbed his chin across the top of her head until their labored breathing had returned to normal. Releasing her, he bent down and kissed the top of each soft breast poised round and firm in the lacy bra.

Hot color invaded her face as Angie fastened the buttons of her silky blouse. She found it amazing that her fingers cooperated, they were trembling so badly.

Simon interrupted her, finishing the task for her. "Do you have anything to drink here?"

She answered him with a slow nod. His gaze followed hers into the miniscule kitchen.

"Sit down, I'll bring us both something."

Angie marveled at his control.

"What does all this tell you, Angie?" he asked as he sat beside her and handed her a drink. She stared at the ice cubes floating on the top of the amber liquid. Bourbon. Oh, dear God, bourbon reminded her of Glenn. Mortification flamed her cheeks all the brighter. She was engaged to Glenn and had allowed Simon to touch her like that. She could have wept with shame.

"Angie?"

"It tells me," she answered forcefully, "that I was a fool to let Glenn talk me into seeing you. I don't want this." Surging to her feet, she stormed across the room to the kitchen and dumped the contents of the drink in the sink. More than at any other time in her life she needed her wits. Being with Simon was enough to cloud her perception without adding alcohol. She thought she saw

Simon's mouth twitch, but when she narrowed her eyes and searched his face, he willingly met her gaze.

"Something is funny?" she challenged.

"I find it amusing that your attitude toward alcohol remains the same. As I recall you were never more angry with me than the night Cal and I got drunk on moonshine."

"You damn near killed yourself."

"I didn't know which was worse," Simon said chuckling, "your outrage or the headache I had the following morning."

"As it happens, I do have an occasional drink. Mostly wine." Her smile was involuntary.

"Good, I'll order a bottle with our meal. Are you ready?"

"In a minute, I'd like to freshen up." Whole lifetimes could pass and she'd never be ready for Simon, not the way he intended.

It took far longer than a minute to repair the damage to her makeup. By the time she reappeared Simon was standing, his drink empty.

He drove to an elegant restaurant situated on a cliff overlooking the Charleston Peninsula. The specialty of the house was lobster, Angie's all-time favorite food. It astonished her that he remembered these minor details about her.

"You remember how much I love lobster."

"There isn't a thing about you that I've for-gotten," he answered as he closed the menu.

135

"Not everything," she said and lowered her gaze. He couldn't. It was impossible.

"I remember that you wanted to name our first daughter after your mother, and we decided on Carolyn Angela Canfield. And we both liked the name Jeffrey, so if it was a boy we'd decided on Jeffrey Simon Canfield. A second boy was to be named Clay. We had it all planned, remember? Two boys and a girl." His voice became low and thick as if it hurt him to recall the intimate details of their early marriage.

They sat across from each other at the narrow table, lost in each other's eyes. Angie didn't want to be sucked into the past and gestured irritably with her hand. "What about you and Carol? Why didn't you have children with her?"

Simon lowered his gaze. "I didn't know if you'd found out about her. I'm glad you did, I wasn't looking forward to explaining it. Marrying Carol was not my most shining hour. There was never any thought of children. We weren't in love."

"Never?" The thought of Simon making love with another woman produced a surge of jealousy that threatened to choke her.

"Never. What about you and Glenn?"

Angie knew instantly what he was asking, but decided to play dumb. "Yes, we're planning to have children. A house full, if Glenn has his say."

Simon blanched. "That's not what I meant."

"It's the only question I'm answering."

The wine steward arrived and began removing the cork from an expensive bottle of Chardonnay. Simon's attention remained riveted on Angie. "Fair enough," he spoke at last. "We won't mention Glenn again."

The meal was the best that Angie could remember. When Simon decided to be charming no one could resist him. Least of all Angie, who had dreamed of shared moments like this.

From the restaurant they drove to a beach. Angie removed her shoes and they walked along the shore as dusk settled over the land. Fresh cool breezes blowing in off the peninsula cooled the evening. Simon attempted to take her hand, but she wouldn't let him. Neither spoke. Angie felt content and melancholy, pensive, and untroubled, desolate and revived as contrasting emotions swarmed at her from all sides. She had to think, to plan. There had to be some way to sort through these emotions. But not now. Not when Simon was at her side and it seemed as if twelve years had fallen away and she was seventeen again and so much in love that all was right in the universe.

"My father has taken a turn for the worse," Simon murmured and looped an arm over her shoulder. She wanted to shrug it free, but discovered she enjoyed the warm, protected feeling it gave her.

Pleased that she let him, Simon paused to drink in the fresh fragrance of her hair and press his cheek to the crown of her head.

"I'm sorry about your father," Angie whispered. Clay, for all his faults, was her only family. If anything happened to him it would devastate her. Angie was uncertain how close Simon was to his father.

"He's been ill for several years now. I don't imagine he'll live another year. I've got to go back, Angie." The appeal in his voice pierced her heart.

"I know."

"Come with me."

"Simon, I can't . . . my life is here now."

"I love you."

Bitter despondency weighed her heart. "I love you, too." Her voice throbbed with the admission. "I don't think I could ever not love you. But that doesn't make things right."

Turning, Simon gripped her shoulders. "Angie, of course it does."

She was close to tears. "We can't go back."

"Why not?" he argued. "I love you, you love me and baby makes three."

"What?" she exploded.

Simon laughed and kissed her brow. "For the first time since I was eighteen, I'm aware of life. This afternoon I took a walk through the park near your shop. Children were laughing and playing and I stood watching their antics, thinking how much I want a child. Our child."

"Simon . . ."

"No." He pressed his forefinger to her lips, silencing her protests. "Hear me out. Two weeks ago if someone had suggested that I'd be talking about a family I would have laughed in their face. I'd given up that dream and a thousand others that we'd planned. I need you. My life is an empty shell without you there to share it with me."

Angie's smile was rueful. "What can I do? My home is here. Clay Pots is here."

"Glenn is here." Steel threads laced his words.

"Yes. You may dislike him, but it was Glenn who forced me to go back to Groves Point."

"You were planning to come anyway or else you wouldn't have wanted to return the money."

"I was going to mail it. Never, at any time did I intend on going back."

"You went to see my mother, didn't you?" That was one thing that had troubled Simon. Georgia Canfield had known from the minute he stepped onto the garden patio the reason for his visit.

"No. She saw me."

"What did she say?"

"Nothing—she just wanted to be sure I wasn't planning on intruding on your life."

Resentment seared through Simon and he squared his shoulders. His jaw was set with implacable determination. "Is she the reason you—"

"No," she assured him quickly. "It's all of it. We accepted it twelve years ago even better than we do now. I'm from Oak Street and you live on Country Club Lane."

"Used to."

"It doesn't make any difference, you understand my point." She broke from his grip and crossed her arms, staring bleakly over the water. Her voice was flat and emotionless when she spoke. "It's time I went home."

Simon was silent on the drive to her apartment, and with each passing second Angie felt her confidence drain out of her. Simon was leaving and she wasn't sure she wanted him to go. And at the same time, with the same heartbeat, with the same breath, she wasn't sure she wanted him to stay.

Simon pulled into the parking lot and turned off the engine. His hands tightened on the steering wheel before he turned and draped an arm over the back of her seat. "I'm not going to pressure you into something you don't want. All I ask is for you to promise me you won't make any decision while I'm away."

They were saying goodbye, at least for now. She was astonished at the wave of bittersweet nostalgia that bordered on sadness.

Intently Simon's eyes were watching her. His

face contained an uncharacteristic appeal that relaxed the firm jawline and faintly curved the chiseled mouth. She released an inward sigh of regret. He was, she mused, all the things a man should be.

Slowly his mouth moved closer to hers. "Promise me, Angie," he said softly, "promise me you won't make any decision when I'm not here."

Instinctively her arms reached for him, her lips parted to receive his kiss. Simon didn't disappoint her. His mouth came down hard with demanding insistence that sent a jarring jolt through her.

"Promise," he whispered, and his tongue plunged into her mouth.

"Simon."

His hand cupped the undersides of her breasts, as he rubbed his thumb over the taut nipples.

"I promise," she whispered, and the shock waves of his touch racked her.

Seven

Angie's dreams were filled with Simon. He satiated her senses until she woke feeling warm, secure and loved beyond measure. It was as though twelve years had been wiped out and she lay content in her bed, knowing Simon would come to her soon and take her to the clearing in the woods. Moisture formed tiny teardrops in the corners of her eyes and slowly spilled onto the pillowcase. When Simon had made love to her, it never failed to move Angie to tears. The experience had been so beautiful that she had cried with joy. Even the first time, when they'd both been innocent, it had been the most poignant experience of her life. Man hadn't created the words to describe the tenderness of that first time. Angie had thought it would be awkward and painful. Instead they had shared a love so ideal, so exquisite, that tears had flowed freely down her cheeks. She had gazed up at Simon in the moonlight and discovered that his face was as moist as her own. They had cried from happiness, their hearts swelling with joy, knowing the love they shared was perfect. It didn't matter what followed in her life, Angie would always treasure that first night in the woods with Simon. The thought of sharing that kind of experience with another man was intolerable. No man could ever reach so deep inside her that he touched her soul. No man could ever love her the way Simon had.

Wrapped in tranquillity, Angie pulled the sheet over her shoulder and snuggled contentedly into the warmth of her mattress. Simon loved her still, and together that love would overcome all the barriers that stretched between them like an impassable mountain range. Together they would forge a pass.

Drop by drop the dream drained from her consciousness, and reality intruded. Angie rolled onto her back and stared sightlessly at the ceiling. Moisture pooled in her eyes and slid haphazardly down her pale face. These tears weren't ones of joy. They had been born of heart-wrenching sadness. A love such as theirs was doomed to face many more difficulties. But Angie had learned long ago that love didn't make everything right. She stood to lose Glenn, and only God knew how her father would react. They'd talk soon and she'd find out. He hated the Canfields, his judgment tainted with the bitterness of his own weakness.

The cost to Simon for loving her would be just as great. His family would never accept her.

Tossing aside the covers, Angie climbed out of bed and reached for the phone. Glenn would want to talk.

A half hour later he was at her front door with a

white bag in tow. "Warm croissants," he said, kissing her on the cheek.

"Coffee?" She rubbed her hands together to chase off a sudden chill.

"Please."

Glenn followed her into the kitchen and pulled out a chair. The look he gave her was long and penetrating, as if he could surmise her feelings with an exaggerated glance. Angie tried to ignore the questions in his eyes. He would wait until she volunteered the information, preferring not to pressure her. Angie didn't know how she could ever hurt a man as good as this one. And she was about to do exactly that.

She set out two plates and delivered steaming mugs of coffee to the table, then took a seat. The white lines of strain about his eyes revealed how tense he was. Waiting for her to tell him what had happened was killing him by inches. Her heart lurched with sadness. He cared for her, and she was about to repay that devotion and patience by crushing him. With a concentrated effort, Angie carefully composed her words.

"Simon and I had a chance to talk last night," she began haltingly.

"Good. I was hoping you would." He blew into the mug before taking a sip.

Angie stared into the black depths of her coffee. "We didn't settle anything. Apparently his father is ill and he couldn't stay."

"So he's gone?"

Angie nodded.

"But not forgotten," Glenn added.

"I don't know if I'd ever be able to forget Simon."

Glenn's hand reached for hers and squeezed it reassuringly. "Angie, I've know that all along. I wouldn't have insisted you see him otherwise."

Angie felt as if the weight of the world had come crashing down on her. "Why are you so good to me?" she pleaded in a low voice.

Glenn chuckled and shook his head. "Do you honestly need to ask?"

Angie swallowed, profoundly touched. "I don't want to hurt you."

His hand continued to squeeze hers. "Loving someone is a strange phenomenon. At least the way I feel about you has taken me by surprise. Your happiness is more important than my own. I'd be lying if I said I wanted to see you and Simon together again. The thought does funny things to my heart, if you want the truth. But I'd never stand in your way if you decided that you do love him and want to share his life."

"Oh, Glenn," she murmured miserably, on the verge of tears. "I don't deserve you."

"But I'm yours," he whispered, lifting her fingertips to his lips and kissing them gently. "No matter what you decide, I'll always be here for you."

●●●

A hundred fifty miles down the road, Simon stretched out his arms as he tightened his grip on the steering wheel. Within three hours he would be back in Groves Point. The six-hour drive would eat up most of the day, but he'd still have time to phone Angie once he arrived home. Lord, he felt seventeen again, happy and carefree. He had the world by the tail and he wouldn't let anyone destroy that happiness. Not again. Not after he'd realized just how much he loved her and always would.

The road felt good beneath him. Everything felt good. The sun was shining and the birds chirped merrily from their lofty perch. For the first time in a lot of years, Simon thought, he was ready to look at life head-on. There was time to appreciate the beauty of the world around him. He had Angie.

When Simon pulled into the driveway, Prince was sleeping on the back steps. Simon's wheels spit up gravel, and he eased his foot onto the brake, coming to a stop. The sleek, black dog was eagerly wagging his tail in greeting. Simon paused only long enough to affectionately scratch the dog's ears before rushing inside the house, taking the back steps two at a time.

The phone number was in his pocket and he dug it out with anxious fingers. Humming, he punched out the number with his index finger, thinking that even the rhythm of her phone number had a musical appeal. He closed his eyes and waited for the soft sound of her voice. Even after all these years it didn't fail to affect him. Heavenly angels couldn't sound more beautiful than Angie.

After several rings Simon hung up, disappointed. He had to hear her voice again, just to know this inexplicable feeling was real and he hadn't imagined it.

Pulling a chair from the kitchen table, Simon straddled it and smiled contentedly. Bringing her the corsage the other night wasn't a brilliant idea. Hell, the woman owned a flower shop. But that wasn't the point. He'd wanted to take them back to the days when she had been his and life had been about as perfect as anyone could expect. The minute she'd seen the flowers, those brilliant eyes of hers had softened and he'd known the time was right to take her in his arms. He had tasted her resistance, but hadn't been persuaded by it. She had probably felt disloyal to Lambert, but she hadn't held back from him long. Simon's spirits had soared and he had realized that without too much difficulty he could have taken her right then. Only the time was wrong and he had known it. No need to rush. She'd felt so soft in his arms, so right. Her body had responded to him as freely as if the years apart had never happened. Simon didn't try to fool himself, he knew Angie hadn't been pleased about that. Just as he had tasted her resistance, he had also been aware of her surprise. She hadn't wanted to feel those things with him. She might even have been testing herself, think-ing she would feel nothing when he held her. Instead, it had been like throwing gasoline on a small fire. The years apart hadn't dulled their bodies' instinctive message to each other.

Simon walked back down to his car and lifted the leather suitcase from the trunk. He deposited it in the bedroom and returned to the kitchen, and opened the cupboard. He should be famished he realized, but a meal without Angie sitting across from him would always make him feel lonely now.

On impulse he tried her line again, holding the earpiece to his shoulder as he checked out the contents of the refrigerator.

"Hello."

Angie's soft voice caught him off guard. "Hello, yourself," he said, straightening. The refrigerator door made a clicking sound as it closed.

"Simon?"

"The one and only."

"Where are you?"

"Home." Good Lord, she had a beautiful voice. She was relaxed, and none of the apprehension he'd heard in their previous phone conversa-tions was evident.

"You must have driven like a madman."

"I got an early start."

She hesitated, and he could feel the tension crackle over the wire as if she were freezing up again.

"How was the drive?" she asked.

"Fabulous. Thinking of you helped pass the time. I told myself I'd play it cool and call you sometime this week. Then I walked right into the house and reached for the phone. I've gone without you for twelve years and suddenly eight hours is more than I can take."

Now she did freeze up. Simon prayed that the day would come when he could speak freely to Angie. But for now he had to be patient.

"Simon, please don't. It's difficult enough keeping everything straight in my mind without you saying things like that."

"But it's true."

"I . . . know, I thought about you, too."

"See," he declared triumphantly. "You love me, Angie. When we're apart nothing is right. We were meant to be together."

She didn't say anything for what seemed an eternity. "Maybe."

Damn, he thought, he shouldn't press her. He knew damn well that Lambert wouldn't. The stockbroker would play his hand carefully and press his advantage when the time was right. Simon had too much at stake to bungle this now.

"I'll make the arrangements to come back next weekend. But this time I'll fly in. That way we can have more time together."

"Okay. By then I should know what I'm going to do. It's not fair to keep you dangling this way."

"I'd wait a lifetime for you, Angie, but don't make me. We've wasted enough time as it is."

Simon hung up, feeling frustrated and irritated with himself. He had to be more patient. Their conversation had started out well, but as soon as he started relaying his feelings, she had become uncomfortable. In future, he vowed, he'd be more careful about what he said.

The late-afternoon sun burst through the window as Angie replaced the telephone receiver. Her heart had soared when she recognized Simon's voice. Even when she'd spent most of the day with Glenn, her thoughts had been on Simon. That stupid dream this morning was the source of that. Even now the memory had the power to disturb her.

Angie clasped her clammy hands together in her lap and stared at the light fixture on the ceiling, taking in several long, even breaths while she tried to clear her thoughts. Her simple life had taken on major complications and there seemed no one who could understand her dilemma.

When her doorbell chimed, Angie didn't need

to guess who was on the other side. Clay almost always stopped in sometime on Sunday, usually around dinnertime.

His look was sheepish as he smiled at his daughter. "Hello, Angelcake." He was a tall man, thin and ungainly. His hair was mostly silver now and receded at the forehead to a sharp W at his hairline. The square jaw dominated his face.

Angie stood on the tips of her toes to lightly kiss his cheek. "I wondered if you'd be coming today."

"Been busy."

"I know." Clay was playing with a new band. For a while he had given up on his music, but his life seemed empty without it, and with Angie's encouragement he had gone back to playing weekend jigs. Although he was involved with music again, Clay had lost his dreams, having long ago abandoned the idea of making it big. He was content to play in taverns and for an occasional wedding. Fewer of those these days.

"I don't suppose you got supper cooking. It's been a powerful long time since I ate a home-cooked meal, you being gone last weekend and all."

Here it was. The perfect opportunity to tell Clay where she had been and whom she had seen, she thought. Her tongue swelled, and her throat went dry. The words refused to come.

"I'll check out the kitchen and see what I can

151

come up with," she said finally. Emotions were warring so fiercely inside of her that for a moment Angie felt like blurting out the truth. Instead she turned toward the kitchen and took the leftover ham from the refrigerator. Cutting off thick slices she placed them in the frying pan.

Chancing a look from the corner of her eye, Angie noticed that Clay was engrossed in the Sunday paper. Misery washed over her and she squeezed her eyes closed.

"Clay."

"Yes?" He lowered the paper.

"I . . . I saw . . ." She paused. "I'm not sure where to start."

"For heaven's sake, girl, spit it out."

Angie braced herself for the backlash. "Simon Canfield was in Charleston this weekend."

Clay gave no outward appearance of having heard her. Angie knew by his look that he was struggling to control his outrage. "And?"

"And what?"

"Did you see him?"

Angie would have thought that much was obvious. "Yes, we had dinner."

With deceptive calmness, Clay laid the newspaper aside and stood. "You had dinner with that bastard after what he did to you?" A muscle leaped in the tightly clenched jaw.

Angie's fingers squeezed around the handle of

the spatula, cutting off the blood supply to her fingers. She forced herself to relax and give the appearance of being calm. "Simon recently learned . . . we . . . we learned that the whole thing was a lie. Simon's mother made up the part about Simon finding someone else. He—"

"Of course he'd tell you that now."

"I believe him."

"Then you're a fool." Forcefully he buried his hands in his pockets.

Angie blanched and turned back to the stove, making a pretense of turning the meat and rearranging it in the pan. A brittle smile cracked her mouth. She hadn't even turned on the burner yet.

There had only been a handful of times in her life that Clay had raised his voice to her. In some ways it was as if their roles had been switched. Oftentimes it was Angie who did the parenting. Clay was the one who needed protecting. Angie forgave him for his weaknesses and loved him for his strengths. He was a rogue who had claimed her mother's heart thirty years ago. Carolyn Robinson had died when Angie was eleven, and Clay's world had shattered. For months he had drifted from job to job like a lost soul seeking his place in eternity. It had been Angie who had held them together, finding excuses for the creditors, smiling calmly at the landlady with the promise that the rent money would be there on Friday. Angie was the one who had insisted they move to Groves Point and settle down. Clay was running, chasing rainbows with his music. They couldn't eat dreams or pay the rent with good intentions. Clay had hated the job at the mill, but it had given them the stability they needed. Soon he had found other musicians and formed a small band. Within six months of settling on Oak Street, he was a semihappy man. At least as happy as he would ever be without his beloved Carolyn.

Clay's attention was riveted on Angie. "What other foolish lies did he feed you?"

"Dad, they weren't lies."

"I thought I raised a smarter girl than this."

"Clay," she protested. "I'll be thirty years old this September. That's old enough to know when someone's telling the truth."

Clay snorted loudly and crossed his arms. "Damn fool, that's what you are—a damn fool."

"Dad." Angie couldn't believe that this was her father talking to her like this. In many ways they were alike. All his life Clay Robinson had loved only one woman. As far as Angie knew he'd lived the past eighteen years celibate.

"I just hope to God that Glenn didn't hear anything about you and that Canfield boy."

"He was the one who encouraged me to meet Simon. In fact, he insisted upon it."

"I can't believe that." Clay continued to pace

154

the confined area of the kitchen in giant, power-filled strides that ate up the distance in two steps.

"Glenn feels that we can't make a future together until we clear away the past."

Clay splayed his fingers through his hair in a jerking movement. "Just how much does Glenn know?"

"Everything."

"Everything!" he exploded. "Only an idiot would have told him how you gave yourself to that rich boy."

"I don't have any secrets from Glenn."

"Well, you sure the hell should have. You gave yourself to him like a shameless hussy."

Angie's head jerked back as if he had physically slapped her with the words. Her fingers tightened around the oven door as she fought to maintain her composure and hold back the tears.

"I'll just pray that you didn't tell Glenn about your so-called marriage."

"He knows that, too."

Clay turned on her with mocking disbelief. "He knows that you behaved like a common tramp and still has anything to do with you?"

"Dad." Angie reeled under the vicious attack of words. "Don't say that."

"Why not? It's true, isn't it?"

The words sliced into her heart like the serrated edge of a knife. This was Clay speaking to her, she reminded herself. But not the lovable roguish father she loved. This Clay was a stranger filled with rage and bitterness. One Angie didn't know or recognize.

"Glenn loves me."

"He must."

Angie's vision blurred until the tall stranger before her became a blurry haze. Somehow she managed to hold back the tears.

"I suppose Canfield claimed undying devotion. That sounds like something those greedy rich folks would do. He couldn't stand the thought of you loving another man." He rammed his hands deep within his pant pockets as he turned toward Angie. "I bet he's kept tabs on you all these years, just waiting for you to find another man. Then the minute you did he popped back into your life, claiming he's always loved you. Ha! The only things those Canfields love is greenbacks."

"I don't believe that." Angie's voice was little more than a hoarse whisper.

"I hope you told him a thing or two."

"No. In fact I'm seeing him next weekend."

Clay looked stunned. "You won't. I forbid it."

Angie's short laugh lacked humor. "It's a bit late for placing restrictions on me, Clay Robinson. I'm a woman now, not a child that you can order about."

Clay's hand gripped the back of the chair as anger contorted his features. "I can't believe my ears. This isn't my Angie talking. You'll do as I say or live to regret it."

"Just what do you plan to do? Lock me in my room or send me to bed without supper?" Angie didn't budge but boldly met his gaze. "You're talking to a woman now. Threats aren't going to intimidate me."

Clay was quiet for an exaggerated moment. "If you so much as speak to that rich boy, then you can forget you've got a father. You hear me, girl? I was fool enough to stand back and let you get involved with him the first time. No more. From now on you're on your own. Understand?"

The thoughts that swam through Angie's mind were ludicrous enough to bring a trembling smile to her lips. She recalled the last time she'd argued with her father. She had been twelve and afraid they were going to be kicked out of the small boardinghouse in which they were living. Clay hadn't paid the rent in two weeks, and no amount of sweet talk was going to persuade the landlady to extend their welcome without payment. At the time Clay was playing the fiddle on street corners, collecting dimes. Angie had been the one to sit her father down and tell him the time had come to look for a job that paid real money. In his usual jovial way, Clay had sung her a song and claimed that a band would come along needing a fiddler and they'd be in Fat City. Angie had shook her head and calmly explained to him that there wasn't any band. They needed money for the rent. She needed new shoes. Clay argued that all he needed was a little time. And twelve-year-old Angie, mature beyond her years, had told him time had run out. Clay had wept bitter tears, wetting her patched dress with his emotion.

"You hear me, girl?" Clay repeated.

"I'm seeing Simon." Composed now, Angie met his gaze without flinching.

"Then you've made your decision. You won't be seeing me again." He stalked from the apartment, slamming the front door as he left.

Crossing her arms to ward off the cold of Clay's departure, Angie slowly shook her head. This had been far worse than anything she would have believed. Clay hated Simon with a bitterness rooted so deep that it had choked off even the most basic reasoning. Given time, Angie was convinced that Clay would come around. She was his daughter, his only child. By tomorrow he'd be back to apologize, she reasoned. When he'd had time to think things through, they would have a reasonable discussion and everything would be made right.

Monday afternoon Angie called Clay before she left the flower shop. Her day had been miserable. The argument had hung over her like a storm cloud from the minute she had climbed out of bed. Even Donna had commented on how unusually quiet Angie was. Clay didn't answer.

Ten tries and five hours later, Angie broke down and drove to Clay's apartment. It was just like him to be stubborn enough not to answer the phone. Fine, she'd face him head-on. This whole affair had gone on long enough. All the family they had in this world was each other. She wouldn't be blackmailed by his demands, but the least they could do was talk things out reasonably.

No light shone through the window of Clay's residence and, after knocking for several minutes, Angie gave up. Reluctantly she returned home, weighted with despair and miserable.

Simon phoned her Tuesday evening, sounding happy and carefree.

"Angie, you won't believe what I did today."

Despite her mood, Angie felt herself drawn into his vivacious happiness. "Tell me."

"Are you sitting down?"

"Should I be?"

"That depends. No, on second thought you wouldn't completely understand this."

"Then tell me."

"I phoned the Y and volunteered to coach basketball next season."

He was right, Angie didn't know why this was such a monumental decision. Simon had always been a talented athlete. It seemed natural that he would share his gift. Maybe, she thought, she was supposed to be surprised that he chose something as common as the Y. "Congratulations."

"I didn't think you'd understand," he said with a chuckle. "Angie, I've holed myself up in my own little world for the past ten years. I've been little more than a recluse. Yes, I played tennis and racquetball and occasionally attended a social function, but it was only the motions of living."

"Simon—"

"Angie," he interrupted, "it's taken me all this time to realize that when you left, something vital in my life went with you: the reason for living."

"Oh, Simon." She felt the thickness building in her throat. When she left, all Simon knew was that she'd taken the money. All he knew was that she'd sold out. It was little wonder that animosity had dominated his life.

"Do you remember that I mentioned watching children play?"

"Yes." Her voice grew soft. Children were her weakness. Clay Pots kept her busy enough to make her forget about the family she'd planned with Simon. Glenn had talked about marriage long before Angie had ever considered it. Only when he mentioned children did he sway her.

"Angie, that was the first time I stopped and noticed children. I couldn't bear to, knowing you and I would never have any."

She closed her eyes and placed a hand over her lips afraid a sob would escape.

"Angie?"

"I'm here," she answered in tortured misery.

The line went silent. "Angie, what's wrong?"

"I'm afraid."

"Oh, love, I am too." For twelve years his life had been in limbo. Now he knew, if Angie chose to marry Lambert, he'd be condemned to hell.

Her throat felt hoarse, but she forced herself to go on. "With the past cleared you'd be able to find another woman to love. I did. Glenn and I were thinking of marriage. In time, you'd do the same."

Her use of the past tense where Glenn was concerned pleased Simon. "Yes," he agreed, not wanting to coerce her into a relationship. "I believe that in time I could. But I'm hoping I won't have to."

That night, Angie lay in bed sleepless. Charleston was hot and humid, and tonight seemed the loneliest of her life. She tried not to think about Simon or Clay or the consequences if she turned away from either of them. Unwillingly she remembered Cindy's words about Simon: an entity unto himself. Simon was independent, he needed no one. And yet he had built a house on the very property that they had once claimed as their own. A house that was little more than an empty monument to a marriage destroyed in its infancy. The house had become testimony to the abject loneliness of Simon's existence. It had looked huge from the outside, and although she'd only been in the kitchen, it had obviously been built with a family in mind. Briefly she wondered if he'd built it when he was married to Carol. Pain seared through her heart. No, she reasoned, from everything she knew of his ex-wife the woman was a social butterfly handpicked by Georgia Canfield. Carol wouldn't have wanted to live outside the social circle of Country Club Lane. The realization eased her mind, but it quickly grew troubled again. The thought of Simon living in the huge house alone was enough to cause tears to gather in her eyes. A part of Simon had never abandoned the hope that she would come back. Dear Lord, how could she ever turn away from this man?

By Wednesday Angie was frantic to know Clay's whereabouts. Every day she phoned the apartment. No one was there to answer, she discovered. Finally Glenn went with her to the tavern where Clay played to patrons who cared little for him or his music. The proprietor claimed that Clay hadn't showed up since Saturday night and that if Angie saw him first, she should tell him there wouldn't be a job waiting for him when he got back.

As he had always done when life became uncomfortable, Clay had run. The rascal, he'd done that to worry her, Angie knew. And succeeded!

"I wouldn't be too concerned. Clay will show up." Glenn placed an arm around her shoulder as they walked back to the car. This was a run-down section of town, poorly maintained. The street light had burned out and without Glenn at her side Angie would have been anxious. Yet, Clay came here night after night.

"He's only doing this to punish me."

Glenn unlocked the car door and held it open for her. "From the look in your eye he's doing a good job."

"He's my father."

"Honey, I know." Solicitously, he squeezed her hand, lending her confidence.

"We were both angry and said things we didn't mean." Angie waited for Glenn to comment about the argument. She'd given him a few details. Just enough for him to surmise what had taken place. Another man would have pressed his advantage, reminding her that if they married, Clay would bless that union. But Glenn remained silent, allowing her to form her own opinions.

They rode silently through the streets back to Angie's place. Glenn stayed only long enough for a cup of coffee. If Clay didn't show up by the weekend, they would look more seriously, he assured her. Glenn had connections. He kissed her lightly and left soon afterward.

Angie was anxiously watching the eleven

o'clock news for reports of unidentified bodies, and hating herself for being so dramatic, when someone rang the doorbell.

Clay stood on the other side, pale and ragged. He didn't look as if he had a decent night's sleep since Sunday. For that matter she hadn't, either. Only Clay looked far the worse.

"Dad." Angie was so relieved to see him that she threw her arms around him and hugged him close. "I'm so glad you're all right."

He simply nodded and patted her back. "Can I come inside?"

"Of course."

He didn't take a seat but clasped his hands in front of him like an errant child. "I guess I've come to apologize for the things I said to you."

"Dad, it's forgotten."

"I'll always love you, Angelcake. But if you decide to have anything to do with the Canfields it'll ruin what we share. Glenn loves you. He's good to you, better than that rich boy ever was."

"It's not that easy." Her voice was low and pleading. She didn't want to rehash Sunday's argument.

"I can't decide for you. But I think you should thank the good Lord for someone like Glenn Lambert. Don't ruin your life a second time."

Angie swallowed back the hurt.

"Now that I've said my piece, I'll be on my

way. The decision is yours. I just wanted you to know I was sorry for the things I said."

"Thank you, Dad." Angie recognized what it had cost him to come to her like this. The argument was the first serious rift in their relationship. Long after he had left, Angie marveled at the depth of this man who was her father.

She tossed restlessly most of the night and waited until nine to phone Simon at the bank. His home number was unlisted. She should have realized people like the Canfields didn't make their phone numbers public.

"Angie." He sounded both pleased and surprised that she'd called. "I tried to catch you last night."

"I was out."

"I know. It was nearly eleven when I quit trying."

"Was there something you wanted to tell me?" *Coward,* her mind screamed. *Tell him now. Get it over with.*

"Nothing in particular. I was going to give you my flight number and—"

"Simon," she interrupted, her eyes closed and her back ramrod straight. "It would be better if you didn't come."

≈ Eight ≈

The force of Simon's shock and anger could be felt through the telephone. "Not come?" His tone demanded an explanation.

"Dad and I had a long talk and—"

"What has your father got to do with you and me?"

Angie pulled out the chair at her desk and sat down, propping up her head with the palm of one hand. "Everything. He's been hurt. He doesn't trust the Canfields and when I told him that I'd seen you—"

"What's the matter, Angie?" Simon cut in bitingly. "Did he think I could fix him up a gig at the country club? Maybe he wanted more money. My mother took delight in telling me how he came back looking for another handout."

Angie gasped, utterly shocked. She sucked in the oxygen so fast her lungs hurt. "That's not true," she cried. "Clay wouldn't do that." Yet, in her heart she knew he had. He'd begged her to go back and demand more money and she had refused. So he'd done it himself. Angie's face burned with sick humiliation. "He didn't mean any harm," she said, her voice cracking. "I'm sorry . . . so sorry," she managed, struggling to keep her voice even. "It should never have happened . . . it won't again." Before she lost her self-control and burst into sobs, Angie hung up the receiver. For a full minute afterward she sat frozen as abject misery washed over her.

Love wasn't supposed to be like this. Love should tear down barriers, build bridges and make everything rosy and wonderful. But in Angie's life it had erected barriers. Walls so high that even the purest forms of love couldn't conquer the granite fortress.

A lone tear weaved its way down Angie's ashen cheek, and she pressed an index finger under each eye to forestall the flood that lay just beneath the surface. Tilting her chin proudly, she bit into her lower lip and sat unmoving until a reassuring calm came over her. She wasn't going to resort to tears. When she turned around and faced Donna, there would be a bright smile on her face.

Somehow Angie managed exactly that, but she didn't fool her astute employee.

"Things sure have been different around here lately," Donna commented as her fingers busily assembled a funeral wreath.

"Oh?" Angie did her best to disguise her feelings. "I can't say that I've noticed."

"Since most of the goings-on involve you, I don't suppose you have," she mocked.

"You're imagining things." Angie, too, found something to keep her hands busy.

"Hmph! Is it my imagination that you jump every time the phone rings, then run to the back of the shop if it's a certain low voice with a long-distance sound? Half the time you come into work looking like you're ready to burst into tears."

"You're exaggerating."

"Could be," Donna asserted, shaking her blond head, "but I see what I see. I figure that I'm going to be making a wreath for you one of these days, but whether it's for a wedding or a funeral I can't rightly say."

Angie's light laugh was decidedly forced.

Later that morning, when she had a free moment, Angie called Glenn at his office to tell him she'd talked to Clay. When Glenn suggested tennis at his club and dinner afterward, Angie agreed readily. The thought of spending another humid night cooped up in the apartment was intolerable.

Simon closed his eyes, cursing himself for having blurted out the fact that Clay had returned to Groves Point wanting more money. His mother had taken delight in informing him of the event. She hadn't needed to elaborate; Simon could well picture the scene. Simon, Senior had handled Angie's father and had made certain the man would never care to return again. It was little wonder Clay Robinson hated the Canfields.

His father could be scathing when the situation called for it, and undoubtedly that one had.

He took another long swallow of his whiskey sour and rubbed a pensive thumb across his furrowed brow. He was going to lose Angie; he could feel it in the pit of his stomach. The acid certainty extended all the way to his heart. She didn't want him to come this weekend and he knew why. That was the worst part. She loved him. But she was going to marry Lambert. After all these years she was unwilling to overcome the differences that separated them. Love wasn't enough for Angie. It didn't conquer the fear.

Another sip of his drink dulled the ache that came with thoughts of her. He remembered holding her in his arms and the way she had melted against him. Her lips had been filled with a sweet passion and although she'd refused to answer his questions about sleeping with Lambert, Simon doubted that she had. Angie was warmth and fire and sweetness and love all rolled into one. And he was going to lose her.

He slammed down his drink and called Prince to his side. Getting out of the house was paramount. Running, walking, anything was better than sitting here tormenting himself. He stood on the top step and looked into the woods. Their woods. A low-lying mist was coming in with dusk, covering the grounds until they resembled a graveyard. Without Angie this place would become little more than that.

His plane was scheduled to leave for Charleston tomorrow evening. He was going to be on it. If Angie was going to choose Lambert, then he wasn't going to make it easy for her. Too much was at stake.

Glenn worked out almost every night at the fitness center. Periodically Angie joined him as his guest. After they were married, he told her, he would add her to the membership. Angie wasn't looking forward to pumping iron and pretending she enjoyed it.

Angie had gone inside to change clothes before meeting Glenn at the outside tennis courts. Glancing around the room at the Nautilus equipment and the trim, muscular bodies of the men and women working out, Angie was reminded that Glenn did indeed love her. If he could spend time each night in the company of these sleek, fine-tuned bodies and then come to her, with all her weak muscles, it had to be love. A set of tennis every week or so was all the exercise she wanted. Working in Clay Pots tired her out enough as it was. The past two weeks had been the worst. Angie felt at her lowest ebb emotionally and physically. Her tennis game showed it.

"Are you sure you're feeling up to this?" Glenn

asked her after she had lost the second game with nary a return.

Angie wiped the sweat from her forehead with a white hand towel. "I have played better tennis."

"My grandmother plays better tennis," Glenn teased. "Why don't we call it quits and get something to eat?"

Angie agreed with a short nod, although her appetite was practically nil.

The hour being early, the restaurant was nearly deserted. No sooner were they seated when a tall blonde waved from across the room and sauntered to their table. Angie self-consciously crossed her legs and ignored the glossily oiled body that claimed the chair next to her. The long-haired beauty had stopped off to say hello to Glenn and proceeded to drape her lithe build over him, making sure he was given the opportunity to admire her ample cleavage. Angie took delight in thinking catty thoughts. The blonde was at least ten pounds underweight. What did it matter if she looked fantastic?

Glenn's glance was apprehensive when the blonde left. "Sorry," he muttered under his breath.

"For what?" Angie's lips twitched with suppressed laughter. "You couldn't possibly believe I'd be concerned that Miss World would turn your head?"

A slow, appreciative smile worked its way across his face as he reached for her hand. "Her beauty pales when she sits next to you." He took her hands and clasped them firmly in his warm ones, his eyes smiling into hers.

"Then the saying that love is blind must really be true."

"Not in this instance. I'm a man who knows what he wants and I want you, Angela Robinson."

The words caught in her throat as she opened her mouth to reassure him that she was his. Instead she looked at him imploringly and miserably lowered her gaze.

"I would have introduced you as my fiancée, but . . ." He let the rest of the sentence fade.

"It doesn't matter," Angie murmured, picking up the menu and focusing her concentration on that. Good grief, did people honestly eat this stuff and live to tell about it, she wondered. A spinach salad was the safest item listed. Angie decided on that and set the menu aside. When she glanced up she discovered that Glenn was continuing to study her closely.

"You say your dad stopped by last night?"

"Shortly after you left." She reached for her water glass and took a long swallow. Even that tasted as if minerals had been added. Determinedly she set the glass aside.

"Is something else bothering you, Angie? You don't look relieved."

"I am, it's just that Clay didn't look well."

"The argument probably had him as upset as you've been the past few days."

"I suppose," Angie drawled, toying with the paper napkin.

"Have you heard from Simon?" Glenn's voice deepened and his eyes grew dark as their gazes locked.

The question caught Angie off guard. Glenn never brought up the subject of Simon. She knew it took great restraint and self-discipline for him to ignore her feelings with the other man.

"I phoned him this morning."

"You called him?"

Angie decided to ignore the implication in his voice. "I asked him not to come this weekend."

Glenn's eyes rounded with surprise, and when he spoke there was a quiet tenderness to his voice that touched her heart. "Does this mean that you're ready to accept my ring, Angie?"

Niggling doubts assaulted her, and she lowered her head as she wondered what madness had overtaken her even to hesitate. Yes, she was ready, as ready as she would ever be where Glenn was concerned. He represented love, security and all the things she'd lacked in her life.

"Glenn . . . I . . ."

"No." His hold on her fingers tightened. "That was unfair. Forgive me."

"Forgive you?" Angie felt a breath away from

insanity. The most wonderful man in the world sat across from her and loved her enough to risk everything, placing her happiness above his own.

"I shouldn't have asked about Simon."

"You have a right."

"No." Slowly, he shook his head, his look thoughtful. "The only rights I have are the ones you give me."

Their conversation was interrupted by the waiter, who came for their order. The moment the man left, Glenn took pains to unfold his napkin and place it in his lap. "You realize he'll come anyway, don't you?"

Angie didn't need to ask whom Glenn was referring to; they both knew. "Yes, I think I do."

Almost immediately Glenn changed the subject, and to Angie's delight he began telling her about his misspent youth in San Francisco. During Glenn's first year of college, his father had been transferred to Charleston, but through the years Glenn had maintained the childhood friendships he'd made in California. With unabashed delight, he relayed several hilarious stories about his high school days and the crowd of young people who were his constant companions. Instantly, Angie's mood lightened. When he told her about his eccentric next-door neighbor, Muffie, she laughed outright.

"Her honest-to-goodness name was Muffie?"

"We called her Muffie because we wanted to muffle her mouth."

"She sounds wonderful, I'd love to meet her someday."

"You will. Some mutual friends of ours are getting married sometime in October. Muffie's the maid of honor and I've been asked to serve as the best man."

Angie liked the way he naturally assumed that she would be with him months into the future. He lent her the confidence she wasn't feeling. "I'll look forward to that."

By the time they left the club the sun was descending into a cloudless blue horizon. Since they had met at the fitness club, Glenn followed her back to her apartment in his car and accepted her offer to come in for coffee.

Angie made the pretense of fixing it for him, knowing it wasn't the coffee that had brought him inside. She filled the brightly colored red kettle with water from the kitchen faucet. A hand at her shoulder stopped her.

"I didn't come here for something to drink," he murmured, turning her into his arms.

Willingly, Angie yielded. Glenn had held her and touched her often over the past several months. Faintly, she recalled that he was taller than Simon and more muscular. Her heart pounded painfully. Why, dear God, why was it that when Glenn held her her thoughts automatically went to Simon? Angry with herself, she looped her arms around Glenn's neck and fit her body intimately to his.

Apparently sensing her need, Glenn kissed her so long and so thoroughly that Angie could almost forget there ever had been a Simon in her life. Almost forget, but not quite.

Angie was struggling over the accounting books Friday afternoon when Donna came to the back of the shop.

"He's here again."

Angie's pencil froze as she glanced at the smiling round face of the yellow clock above her desk. Simon was earlier than she had expected. He must have caught the earliest commuter plane, which left Groves Point early in the afternoon, she thought distractedly. Mentally she had prepared herself for this.

"He asked me to give you this." Donna set a small white box on top of the desk and returned to the front counter.

Angie's heart pounded so loudly her ears hurt with the hammering vibrations. Sluggishly and with extreme caution, as if she were handling something radioactive, Angie picked up the box. He wouldn't. Dear heavens, he wouldn't. Her fingers were trembling so badly she paused before removing the lid, biting her lip as she did. Emotion engulfed her as the tears pooled in her eyes. She struggled with the emotion and managed to hold at bay the moisture that clouded her vision.

The ring. Fleetingly she had wondered how long it would take Simon to play his trump card. The simple gold band with the tiny diamond had cost him far more than the money involved. He had saved for it out of the monthly allowance his father sent to him at the university. Simon had sacrificed to buy her the ring, going without the little things that would have made his life away from home more comfortable. The wedding band had been his Christmas present to her, and he'd made small monthly payments on it long after she had left Groves Point. The day Georgia Canfield had given Angie the money, she had handed his mother the small white box and asked that she return it to Simon. During all these years, Simon had kept the ring.

"Do you remember the night I gave you the ring?" His low, enticing voice came from behind her.

"No," she lied, angry and unreasonable. It was unfair that he do this to her. No woman would forget a night like that. They couldn't be together Christmas Day because of Simon's family, so he had come to her late Christmas Eve with the box wrapped and hidden in his jacket pocket.

Angie had been so delighted that the lump in her throat had prevented her from speaking. Only that lump had been one of intense happiness.

"Don't you think it's time I gave my wife a wedding ring?" Simon had whispered in her ear. His gray eyes had filled with love and adoration as he slipped his class ring from her finger and replaced it with the small diamond. Later they had made love with an aching tenderness that stole her breath away. After so many weeks apart, Angie had assumed their lovemaking would be hot and urgent. Instead, Simon had loved her with a reverence, holding her so close Angie had been convinced that nothing could ever come between them. Not parents, not a whole town, not even God Himself. The beauty of their lovemaking was so profound that tears had shone in her eyes. With his arms wrapped securely around her, Simon had whispered the most beautiful words, his voice hoarse with tenderness. He murmured all the words a woman longs to hear, telling her of the unchanging love represented in that ring. He asked her to wear it proudly as a symbol of his devotion to her.

Clay had noticed the ring soon after Christmas, gleefully assuming that Angie and Simon were engaged. In her innocent happiness, Angie had told her father about what she and Simon had done that summer in the church. Clay wasn't pleased and Angie regretted having told him anything.

"Angie," Simon spoke again. "You remember, just as I remember that Christmas."

"Why did you keep it?" She was amazed that the squeaky high voice was her own.

"You forget that for three years I waited for you to come back."

"But I didn't." She held her back rigid.

"Yes, you did, only it took longer than three years. You've come back to me now, Angie."

"You're forgetting something," Angie murmured tightly. Her fingers were clenched fast to the box, and she mentally ordered them to relax before she set it aside. "You're forgetting Glenn."

"I haven't forgotten anything." He placed his hand on her shoulder and his touch was like a slow fire that moved insidiously toward her heart, searing a trail as it traversed. "Angie, look at me," he requested on a husky murmur.

Slowly she turned the desk chair around, keeping her eyes focused on the tiled shop floor. Tenderly, Simon lifted her eyes to his and drew her gently to her feet, taking both her hands in his.

"I've been away for six long days." He wrapped his arms around her waist and brought her close. "Welcome me back, love. Tell me you missed me as desperately as I missed you."

Angie felt like a rag doll, powerless to resist Simon. She didn't want to kiss him and yet she knew that nothing on this earth would prevent what was about to happen. Very slowly she slid her hands over his chest and pressed her mouth to his. Immediately, Simon deepened the kiss.

Angie drew his tongue into her mouth and offered him hers. Simon groaned and leaned against her. Gently, Angie laid her slender fingers over his cheek and her mouth clung to his, moving back and forth in passionate surrender, aroused fully by the wildly erotic kiss.

Simon stroked her hair, weaving his fingers in and out of its glorious length as his mouth slanted over hers in a lingering kiss that left them both panting and breathless.

"Oh, love," he half laughed and half groaned on a long, unsteady breath. "That kiss was worth a six-day wait."

Angie buried her face in the open throat of his shirt and shivered with confused delight when he pressed her so close to his hard length that it felt as if their bodies were fused together. "Oh, my sweet Angie," he groaned into her hair. "I've gone twelve years without you, and a minute more demands all the restraint I can muster." There was an unmistakable quaver in his voice.

Angie was experiencing many of the same sentiments. Knowing that Simon had saved the wedding ring had pushed her over the brink.

"Please, Simon, this shouldn't have happened." It took a great effort to keep her voice steady. "Not here."

He lifted her chin and kissed her lightly on the lips. "All right. Your place or mine?" His eyes sparked with mischief.

Righteously she broke from his embrace, fighting back the sudden urge to laugh.

He took her hands in his and leaned back to study her, as if seeing her for the first time. Several electrifying minutes passed before either of them spoke.

"Have dinner with me tonight?"

"No." Angie shook her head and lowered her gaze. "I can't."

"Can't." His grip on her fingers tightened painfully. "Is it Lambert?"

"I asked you not to come this weekend."

"You honestly didn't expect that would keep me away, did you?" He was angry now and struggling not to reveal how much.

"Glenn knew it wouldn't . . . I guess I'd hoped."

"What exactly were you hoping?"

Angie had edged up against the desk so that the sharp rim cut into the back of her thighs. "I wish you hadn't come."

"You couldn't have proved it by me just now."

"We have . . . a physical thing." She tried desperately to play down the attraction between them.

"Is that a fact?" he demanded furiously. "And do you share this attraction with Lambert as well?"

"Yes," she lied, her heart throbbing painfully with the deceit.

Simon stiffened and held his body so tense that Angie was convinced he couldn't breathe. The battle waging within showed plainly on his face. His eyes narrowed fractionally, and one side of his mouth twisted cynically. He didn't want to believe her and at the same moment didn't know if he dared not.

"I see," he spoke at last.

Angie's legs felt as if they were water, and she leaned her weight against the desk, praying it would keep her upright until she'd finished. "You asked me to make my decision," she began in a voice that trembled so hard she wondered if Simon could understand her.

"You promised not to until I was here."

"You're here now." She gestured weakly with her hand. "You will always be someone special in my life. You were my first love, and for a lot of years I didn't think I could ever love again. Glenn taught me that I could."

"Angie—"

"No," she cried desperately, "let me say what I have to, otherwise I may not have the courage to do it and the whole thing will drag out the agony."

Simon's eyes were so hard that they sliced directly into her. His jaw was clenched so tight that his face went white. Slowly, as if he couldn't bear to look at her another minute, Simon closed his eyes.

"Things would never work for us, Simon. I've thought it all out. That you could still love me is the greatest honor of my life. In the years to come

I will always remember you with a fondness—"

"Fondness." His control snapped. "Save that weak, insipid emotion for your precious Glenn."

Her heart slammed against the wall of her chest at the pain she was inflicting upon them both. Her eyes ached with unshed tears, and she bowed her head unable to look at him. "Simon, I'm so sorry," she whispered and nearly choked, ". . . so sorry."

Angie wasn't sure what she expected. Her thought was that he would try to inflict the same kind of pain on her with bitter words or cruel accusations. The last thing she had thought he would do was laugh. Admittedly the chuckle was mirthless and devoid of amusement, but it caught her by surprise and she raised her eyes to his.

"I let you walk out of my life once and I'm not about to make that mistake again," he taunted.

"Simon—"

"You've had your say, now listen to me. More than anything that's happened in the past couple of weeks, you just proved how much you do love me."

"That kiss was—"

"Not the kiss, Angie, but your reaction to it. It scared you. You couldn't possibly love another man as much as you do me. I don't believe it's in you to marry a man you love less."

"I'll learn," she cried.

Simon was gambling and knew it. He struggled not to reveal his fear. "I know you. In some ways better than you know yourself. You wouldn't cheat Glenn by marrying him when you feel this strongly for me. And you do love me, Angie, so much it's nearly killing you."

"It won't work with us. Can't you accept that?"

"We'll make it work," he argued. "Go on—run away, marry Glenn if you think you can, salvage your father's pride, but I'll follow you. There won't be a minute of any day that I won't haunt you, because I'll be waiting for you, Angie, in Groves Point where you belong, where we belong."

"Simon . . ."

His mouth came down hard, silencing Angie. Her mind screamed a warning as her emotions reeled and waves of longing racked her. She tried to push herself free, but he wouldn't let her, holding her fast. His mouth softened, stroking hers with a gentleness until she mentally acknowledged that she had lost. Her mouth parted helplessly beneath his. The very hands that had pushed against his chest seeking freedom, now slid convulsively around his neck, clinging to him. Wildly she returned his kiss, on fire for him, loving the feel of his body rasping against her soft breasts. Abruptly she was free. Reeling under the shock, Angie swayed until a hand at her shoulder righted her and she gained her balance.

"You think of me, Angie, waiting," he murmured, his voice raw with emotion. For interminable seconds he stood staring at her, as if studying every line of her pale face, drinking his fill before the self-imposed thirst.

Angie didn't move, didn't breathe. The four walls closed threateningly in around her, blocking her vision. Before she could utter a word to bid him stay or leave, Simon was gone.

Angie didn't know for how long she stood rooted and unable to move. Simon was right. She couldn't marry Glenn. To do so would be cheating him of the kind of wife he expected and needed.

With confused, sorrowful brown eyes, Angie stared ahead at the road that stretched before her. All she could see was a life of loneliness.

❧ Nine ❧

"You haven't seen that Canfield boy again, have you?" Clay asked a week after Simon had left Charleston. They sat around Angie's small kitchen table on a lazy Sunday evening, eating lemon meringue pie. Clay's favorite.

"No." Angie cast a pleading glance in Glenn's direction. His hand reached for hers and held it firmly in a warm clasp.

"Angie won't be seeing anyone but me from now on," Glenn said, and his eyes glowed with a triumphant happiness.

Angie had spent long and difficult hours sorting through Simon's parting words. He was right, she did love him. Nothing could change that. The years hadn't diminished the intensity of her feelings and she realized she shouldn't expect time to ever gloss them over. But that didn't have to ruin her life. Glenn loved her, really loved her. Enough to accept the fact that her feelings might never be as strong as his.

Clay pushed his half-eaten pie aside and dabbed the edges of his mouth with the paper napkin.

Not for the first time, Angie examined her father's unnaturally pale features. "Are you feeling okay, Dad?"

He looked surprised that she would notice.

"I've been having these funny pains lately. Nothing serious, but I been thinking about seeing a doctor."

In twenty-nine years Angie had never known her father to admit he wasn't feeling up to par. Not once could she ever remember him visiting a physician. For years Clay had blamed the medical profession for her mother's death and claimed that all doctors were crooks.

"Would you like me to make an appointment for you?" She broached the subject carefully, not wanting to appear overly concerned.

"Maybe you should."

"I'll do that tomorrow then." Worried, Angie looked to Glenn for support and found his eyes studying Clay. Glenn's features were drawn with concern.

"I think I'll be headin' home," Clay announced, pushing against the table and scooting out his chair. "I'm feeling a mite under the weather."

"I'll go with you," Glenn offered, dumping his napkin on the table beside his plate.

"No reason for that," Clay scoffed. "What I'm really doing is giving you two younguns time alone. A boy like you should be smart enough to see that."

"In that case," Glenn said with a chuckle, delivering his plate to the sink, "I'll put the time to good use."

Angie walked her father to the front door and

felt his forehead. Annoyed, Clay brushed her hand aside. "I ain't that sick. Now you get back in the kitchen with Glenn and give me a call tomorrow, you hear."

But behind his words, Angie sensed an underlying fear. There was something wrong, and Clay was both worried and confused. Agreeing to a doctor appointment proved as much. "Yes, Daddy dearest," Angie murmured solicitously and kissed him lightly on the cheek.

"Have you two set the date yet?" Clay whispered, glancing into the kitchen. "I've been doing a lot of thinking lately. It seems time I was bouncing a grandbaby on my knee. I might even compose a lullaby or two."

Angie stiffened. The pressure was on her from both Glenn and Clay to set a wedding date. As it was Angie had yet to accept Glenn's grandmother's ring. Her emotions were too unsettled to leap into a rushed engagement and marriage. She needed time and both Glenn and Clay were growing impatient. "Not yet."

"You aren't still hankering after that rich boy?"

Angie had been "hankering" after Simon Canfield since she was a high school junior. She shook her head. "No, Clay," she lied. "I'm over Simon Canfield."

"Good." His low hiss was filled with relief. "You won't be seeing him again?"

"No."

"He's not coming to Charleston?"

Angie felt like screaming. Why did Clay insist on dragging this inquisition out? "No."

Clay wiped a hand across his wide brow. "For all our sakes I hope so," he said and turned into the night. Angie stood at the door watching the dejected figure as he turned into the parking lot.

Glenn had cleared the dinner dishes from the table by the time Angie returned. She paused, deep in thought, and gripped the back of a chair.

"I'm concerned about Clay." Glenn spoke first. "I'd bet you anything those little pains of his are a lot more than little."

Angie agreed with an abrupt nod, worried herself. "I'll make an appointment for him in the morning."

"I'd suggest he see an internist."

"What do you think it is?" Angie turned imploring eyes to Glenn, fear playing havoc with her composure.

"I don't know, honey. I'm not a doctor."

Angie nodded, fighting down a sense of panic. For all his weaknesses Clay was still her father and her only living relative.

"I've got the coffee poured," Glenn announced. "Let's sit in the living room."

"Fine," Angie agreed, following him into the room. They sat so close on the blue velvet sofa that their thighs touched. Relaxed, Glenn stretched his long legs out in front of him and crossed his ankles. He draped an arm over the back of the sofa. "Is there anything interesting on TV tonight?"

Angie flipped through the pages of the *TV Guide* and shook her head. "The usual."

His hand cupped her shoulder and moved slowly down the length of her arm. Angie closed her eyes, wanting desperately to feel the comfort of his touch.

"Dinner was wonderful," Glenn whispered and gently kissed her temple.

"Thank you, but I hardly think of fried chicken as wonderful. Wait until you taste my Shrimp Diane."

"I'll look forward to that."

Involuntarily, Angie stiffened. It was coming, she could feel it in every breath Glenn drew. He wanted to talk about getting married and her mind was devoid of arguments.

"Sitting here watching television after a big Sunday dinner seems natural," Glenn said, setting his coffee aside.

"Yes, it does," Angie agreed.

"Like folks who've been married for years and years."

"Yes." The lone word barely made it through the growing thickness in Angie's throat.

"You know how I feel about you, Angie. I've waited so long for you. I don't want to lose you now."

"You're not going to lose me," she argued, straightening. Turning, she looped her arms around his neck and pressed her cheek against his throat. "Be patient with me just a while longer." She paused to lightly kiss his Adam's apple.

Glenn's arms tightened around her. "How much longer?" Disappointment coated his voice.

"I . . . I don't know."

"Two weeks, a month, six months?" he pressed.

"I don't know." She squeezed her eyes closed, hating herself for doing this to someone as wonderful as Glenn.

"When will you know?"

"Soon," she promised. "Soon."

A finger under her chin lifted her face to his. For a long moment, Glenn gazed into the dark depths of her troubled eyes. His voice was deep and velvety as he spoke. "I want you, Angie." Slowly, enticingly, his mouth inched closer to hers and stopped just when she felt he could go no nearer without touching. "Don't hold back from me, love."

Angie saw the look in his eyes and a warning screamed along the ends of her nerves. Glenn wanted to love her completely. He was finished with having her so close and being denied what he craved most. For her own part she could see no reason to hold back from Glenn. She had shoved Simon from her life—oh, Lord, it was happening again, she groaned inwardly. Glenn took her into his arms and her thoughts flew to Simon.

Filled with self-loathing, Angie twined her arms around Glenn's neck and eagerly parted her mouth to his.

"Oh, love," Glenn groaned and hungrily devoured her waiting lips. Urgently, his hands moved down her shoulders and back, molding her to his upper torso. His kisses were insistent, thorough and seemingly endless. His probing tongue parted her lips and plunged inside, seeking to mate with hers. Tentatively she touched the tip of it to his and felt him go weak against her. Moaning, his arms crushed her, seeking a greater fulfillment.

Angie's resolve to finally give in to Glenn splintered with every kiss, every caress. She longed to be warm and yielding, gifting him with the love he deserved. He had been patient with her, and soon she was going to be his wife. Yet she felt paralyzed with alarm, bewilderment and even shame, as if she were contemplating something as appalling as adultery.

When his hands sought her ripe breasts, Angie submitted docilely, but when he pulled at the elastic waistband of her summer shorts, her startled eyes flew open.

"Glenn," she whispered, not knowing how to deal with this new invasion.

He didn't seem to hear her, kissing her with flaming demand. Angie squirmed and jerked Glenn's hand free. Undeterred, he continued kissing her while fiddling with the buttons of her blouse.

Weakly, Angie submitted, not knowing how to stop him as he slipped the polished cotton cloth from her shoulders. Instantly his fingers sought to release her lacy bra.

"Glenn." She pleaded with him, but her voice was little more than a strangled whisper. "Don't, please."

He silenced her with a kiss, grinding his lips over hers until there was no fight left in her. Angie didn't try to free herself, but weakly submitted, not touching him as she surrendered helplessly to his brutal possession of her mouth.

When he finally drew back, Angie's forehead fell against his chest. Her hands were flattened against his crisp shirt. She felt disoriented, frustrated and so bewildered. Tears filled her eyes and crept down her pale face.

"Angie," he pleaded, "did I hurt you?"

He loved her, urgently wanted her to be his wife, and she'd turned him away from the very things he should expect. Yet he wanted to know if he had hurt her. The realization produced a flood of tears. She buried her face in her hands and wept bitterly.

"Oh, God, Angie, I'm sorry." He wrapped his arms around her, holding as if she were a child. He pressed a brief kiss on the crown of her head and rocked her in a gentle swaying motion. "I wouldn't hurt you for anything in the world."

"Glenn," she cried. "I'm the one . . ."

"Shhh." He kissed her again. "No, it was my fault, I shouldn't have pressed you."

"But I don't think I'll ever feel differently."

"Yes, you will," he whispered confidently. "In time, love. In time."

Angie couldn't get Clay an appointment for the internist until the middle of the week. She picked him up at his place and was shocked at his drawn, ashen features. For half a minute she toyed with the idea of taking him directly to the hospital emergency room, but the receptionist had gone to a lot of trouble to squeeze Clay in for the last appointment of the day. Wordlessly she drove to the doctor's office, chatting to keep her mind off how worried she was.

The time in the waiting room while Clay was with the doctor seemed interminable. Angie leafed through the magazines with unseeing eyes and checked her watch every few minutes. After an hour, she began pacing the deserted room. What could possibly be taking so long?

The receptionist appeared moments later. "The doctor would like to see you in his office."

"Of course." Angie's stomach had coiled into a hard knot by the time she shook hands with the doctor and sat in his compact office.

"I'd like you to take your father directly to the hospital."

Angie scooted to the edge of the woven beige cushion. "What's wrong?"

"Don't alarm yourself. There are a few tests I'd like to run. Unfortunately, he seems adverse to the idea."

"My . . . my mother died in a hospital." Angie knew how inane that sounded, but it was the only thing she could think to say. "Don't worry, doctor, I'll get him there."

Saying she'd deliver Clay to Charleston General and doing so proved to be a formidable task.

"I'm not going to any hospital," Clay announced stubbornly.

"Yes, Clay," she agreed blandly.

"I mean it."

"Yes, Clay."

Angie started the engine of the car and eased into the evening traffic.

"This isn't the way to my house."

"I know."

"You're taking me to that hospital, aren't you?"

"Yes, I am. You can shout, scream and do anything else you want, but you're going to that hospital."

"Angie, don't. I'm begging you, girl. You take me there and I won't ever walk out. Mark my words. If I'm going to die I want to be in my own bed with my own things around me."

"You're not going to die, you understand," she cried, pressing back the growing fear. "I won't let you. Now quit your arguing."

"You're killing me as surely as if you'd stuck a knife in my heart. You're sentencing me to die."

"Stop it right now, Clay Robinson. The doctor said that he was only sending you there for a few tests. You'll only be there a couple of hours. Then I'll take you home."

"You promise me?"

The doctor had mentioned the possibility of admitting Clay, depending on the test results. "I promise that you're going for tests."

"But you won't let them keep me, will you?"

"We'll see."

"Angie." Clay doubled over in the front seat, gripping his stomach. "Oh, God, the pain. I can't take it."

Angie's hand tightened around the steering wheel. "I'm hurrying, Dad. We'll be there in a minute." Pressing on her horn, Angie wove in and out of traffic, driving at breakneck speed. She pulled into the emergency entrance and rushed inside for help. Two men with a stretcher raced to her car and jerked open the passenger door. By the time they arrived, Clay was writhing with agony. He tossed his head to and fro and flung his arms out like a madman.

"Angie," he cried pitifully. "Don't let them take me."

"Daddy." She gripped his hand. "You're sick, they only want to help you."

He squeezed his eyes shut. "They're taking me to my death."

The two attendants stopped her from going inside the emergency room cubicle. Angie came to a halt outside the room and leaned against the wall, needing its support to remain upright. Clay was right. He was going to die and there wasn't anything she could do about it. She wiped the tears from her face and smiled gratefully to the nurse who led her to a seat in the waiting room. What seemed like hours later, but could have been only a few minutes, a doctor approached her.

"I'm afraid your father will require emergency surgery."

"Why?"

"He has diverticulitis."

The word meant nothing to Angie. "Will he be all right?"

The doctor hesitated. "We'll let you know as soon as we do. If you'd like you can see him for a few minutes before we take him upstairs."

"Yes, please." Angie followed the doctor into the cubicle. Clay lay with his eyes closed on the stretcher-bed, his face as pale as the sheets and marked with intense pain.

"Clay," she whispered, reaching for his hand and kissing his fingers.

He rolled his head to the side and tried to smile. "I want you to remember that I always loved you, Angelcake. You were the light of your mother's and my world."

"Daddy, don't talk like this."

"Shhh . . . a man knows when he's going to die." He was so calm, so sure. "I'm ready to meet my Maker. . . ." His voice faded. ". . . lots of regrets . . . loved you."

As the hours passed, Angie grew as certain as Clay that this day would be his last. And with the certainty came the realization that there was nothing she could do. She prayed, pleaded, bargained with God to spare her father. Forcing happy thoughts into her troubled mind, she recalled the times as a little girl that he'd sung her to sleep and made up jingles just for her. He'd tugged her pigtails and called her his Angelcake. She remembered how desolate Clay became after her mother's death and knew she would feel the same without this roguish old man to love. He was a rascal, a scoundrel, a joy and a love, all in one. Life wouldn't be the same without him. He was her link to the past and her guide to the future. And he was dying.

Sweat outlined the greenish-blue surgical gown the doctor wore when he approached Angie several hours later. She could see from the disturbed frown that marred his face that his news wasn't good.

Linking her hands together, Angie slowly rose to her feet, bracing herself for the worst.

"I'm sorry," he said softly, "we don't expect him to last the night."

Angie's head jerked back as if the man had physically struck her. "Can I see him?"

"In a few minutes.

"Is there someone you'd like to call?" he asked her gently.

Blankly Angie stared at the exhausted man. Clay hadn't been to church in years. There was no one in all the world she wanted now, save one.

"Yes, please," she murmured, her voice barely audible. The card he'd given her was in her purse. The phone number was inked across the printed surface of the business card. For several exaggerated seconds she stared at the telephone dial, knowing what it would mean if she called.

He answered on the sixth ring. "Yes?"

"Simon," she whispered, trying to gain control of her voice. "Clay is dying. I need you."

Ten

The early light of dawn had washed away the dark, lonely night. Angie sat beside her father's hospital bed, pressing her forehead against the cold, metal railing, fighting off the enfolding edges of exhaustion. Clay remained unmoving, his head lolled to one side as he battled for each breath. Nurses moved in and out of the room with silent steps as they checked Clay's vital signs and marked their findings on the metal clipboards they carried.

Sunlight crept through the slits in the blinds, and the nurse quietly turned them completely closed. Angie yearned to tell her that she wanted Clay to die with the sun in his eyes. But it took more energy than she could muster just to speak. Instead she waited until the woman had left the room, and then she stood, intent on opening the blinds and flooding the room with glorious light.

"Angie." Simon's husky voice stopped her.

An overpowering surge of relief washed over her as she turned to him. They met halfway into the private room, reaching out to each other like lost souls released from a hellish trap. Simon's arms surrounded her, and he lifted her feet from the floor as he buried his face in her hair.

"Thank you," she whispered chokingly over

and over. Her body shook violently as she clung to him with the desperation of a drowning woman.

"Angie," he answered. "Tell me what happened." Simon's gaze drifted to the unearthly pale face of the man on the bed. For all his differences with Clay Robinson over the years, Simon felt a stirring sense of loss. Angie and her father had always been close, and her grief affected him now more than he would have believed. Her softly murmured phrases were unintelligible and he could do little more than smooth the hair from her brow and hold her close to his warmth.

The doctor arrived, and Angie and Simon stepped outside the room while the middle-aged man with the serious, dark eyes examined Clay.

Angie's hand held Simon's in a tight grip as if she were afraid that he would leave her. If it were up to Simon they would spend the rest of their lives together, starting at this moment.

"Dad had diverticulitis."

Simon blinked and repeated the words. "What does it mean?"

"I'm not sure I know exactly, but from what the doctor explained the intestines have tiny sacs along the outside edges. When the diet doesn't include enough roughage these sacs can fill and become infected. That's what happened to Clay. His infection was so advanced that the sacs were filled and ready to burst. If they had, he'd be dead now. As it is . . . his chances aren't good." She paused and ran her fingertips along the hard, sculptured line of his jaw. "How did you get here?"

"Drove." He didn't add that he hadn't stayed under the speed limit the entire way. The desperation in Angie's voice had affected him like nothing he had ever known. Angie had always been the strong one in any crisis. People leaned on her. From the time they were in their teens, Simon had marveled at the way others sought her out with their problems. Now in her own grief, Angie had turned to him. Simon's heart pounded at the profound comfort he found in that. She hadn't called on Glenn, who was so close and who would have been so willing. She had reached out to him.

"Oh, Simon, I'm so sorry to put you through this."

"Don't be." He took her in his arms again, unable to keep from holding her. "I tried to catch a commuter plane, but the first one wasn't due out until this afternoon." He didn't mention the fruitless time spent trying to locate a private plane and pilot. "I'm here now and I'm staying. That's all that matters."

"The doctor didn't think Clay would last the night, but he has. That's a good sign, don't you think?"

She was pleading with him like a small child,

as if it were in his power to change the course of fate. Gently he kissed her temple. "Yes, I think it must be." The sight of the old man had shook Simon. The Clay Robinson on the bed was barely recognizable as the man Simon had known. Clay had aged drastically in the past twelve years. His hair was completely gray now, and the widow's peak was more pronounced. His skin color was beyond pale, a grayish hue of a man just on the other side of death. Simon ached with compassion for Angie; his heart surged with the need to protect her from this.

When the doctor reappeared, Simon slipped his arm around her shoulder and held her protectively to his side.

"He made it through the night," Angie said eagerly, the grip on her emotions fragile.

The doctor's returning smile was tight. "Yes, he's surprised us all."

"How much longer will it be before we know?"

"It could be days. I suggest you two go home and get some rest. The hospital will contact you if there's any change in Mr. Robinsons's condition."

Angie turned stricken eyes to Simon, communicating her need to remain at Clay's bedside. "Would it be all right if we stayed a while longer?" Simon asked.

"If you wish. Only I don't think it's necessary to continue a twenty-four-hour vigil. Mr.

Robinson is resting comfortably now. I doubt that his condition will change over the next several hours. At this point I'd say we are optimistically hopeful for his recovery."

"Thank you, Doctor," Angie whispered fervently, her trusting dark eyes filling with tears of gratitude.

"No need to thank me. I can do only so much, the rest remains with God and your father."

Together the couple returned to Clay's room. With Simon on the other side of the bed, Angie sat across from him, her hand gripping the railing as if needing to hold on to something tangible in a sea of uncertainty.

Simon coaxed her once to get something to eat, but she refused with a hard shake of her head. Her hand clasped Clay's and she whispered soothingly as if her words would give him comfort. Gradually her head began to droop, and eventually she propped it up against the back of her hand as it gripped the metal barrier.

"Come on, Angie," Simon spoke softly, taking her by the shoulders. "Let me drive you home. You need your rest. We'll come back later."

Rubbing the sleep from her face, Angie yawned and slowly shook her head. She'd been awake for over thirty-six hours and was so rummy that she would have agreed to anything. Simon was here. She trusted him. Simon would take care of everything.

He helped her stand, and she leaned her cheek against his chest as he looped an arm around her shoulders, leading her to the parking lot and into the bright light of day.

The sun was shining and reflected off the hood of his sports car as Simon drove down the busy Charleston streets. Most of the traffic was heading for the downtown area, and since they were traveling in the opposite direction, toward Angie's apartment, they weren't hampered by rush hour.

Once inside the apartment, Angie flipped the switch to the air conditioner. Immediately a shaft of cooling air weaved its way through the apartment.

"You go ahead and get ready for bed, I've a few phone calls to make," Simon said softly. He wanted to contact the flower shop so they wouldn't worry about Angie not showing.

His words barely registered as Angie moved into her bedroom and began stripping off her blouse and slacks. She glanced longingly into the bathroom and decided to shower.

Simon heard the running water and paused to rub the exhaustion from his eyes. While waiting for Angie he discovered that the hall cupboard held an extra set of bedding. He'd get whatever sleep he could on the sofa when the opportunity presented itself.

Spreading the sheets for his makeshift bed,

Simon felt a great weight ease from his heart. These past days apart from Angie had driven him to the brink of insanity. The agony of walking away from her with nothing more than a few parting words had filled him with regrets. His mind had ached like a throbbing bruise that didn't lessen with time, taunting him. Like Lambert, Simon had gambled. Clay's illness had hastened Angie's ultimate decision, but Simon had realized the minute he picked up the phone and heard her voice that she would never leave him again. She was his and would always be his alone.

The sound of running water stopped and Angie reappeared, standing just inside the living room. The thin nylon gown was lilac colored. Simon's breath stopped short, causing an aching shortness in his lungs. She was so exquisitely beautiful that he slowly straightened, unable to tear his gaze from her. Her breathtaking loveliness reminded Simon of the way she'd come to him in the clearing in the woods. The neckline of the gown formed a deep V to reveal the pale valley between her breasts, and she stood there waiting for him as innocent as spring. Simon recognized that he couldn't abuse her trust.

"Simon," she whispered and held out her hand. "Don't sleep on the sofa."

Briefly he closed his eyes to the gnawing ache in his loins. She couldn't possibly expect him to go to bed with her and not touch her. Dear Lord, he couldn't take her now! Not with Clay on his deathbed and Angie distraught and confused. Yet he didn't know if there was anything he could refuse her.

"Here, let me tuck you in." He struggled to keep his voice cool and impersonal and crossed the room, not daring to look at her.

Her bedroom was small and dominated by the bed and dresser. Her slacks and blouse were neatly folded across the foot of the mattress. Simon turned back the covers and fluffed up the pillow. "There," he said, "your bed awaits you, my lady." Again he avoided looking directly into those soulful, dark eyes as she slipped between the crisp sheets. Wordlessly he pulled the covers over her shoulders and tucked them under the lip of the mattress as if he were putting a small child to bed.

Angie cast him a look of mild surprise and he noticed that some color had returned to her pale face. "Simon," she said in a low, husky voice. "Could you . . . would you mind lying down with me? I don't want to be alone."

Simon felt like gnashing his teeth. She had no conception of what she was asking of him. "Sure." He removed his shirt and trousers and slid between the sheets beside her. The narrow bed that forced her to scoot her thinly clad body close to him was an additional torture. He gathered her in his embrace, and closed his eyes to the agony of being so near her. Breathing in the fresh scent of her hair, Simon held himself completely still. He tried not to think of the satin feel of her ivory smooth skin and forced himself to concentrate on anything but the warm, vital woman in his arms.

Angie sighed contentedly, not completely unaware of what she was doing to Simon. Maybe it was selfish to use him this way, she thought sleepily, but she couldn't help herself. Today more than any time in her life she needed him. Dreamily, she smiled up at him and nestled in his embrace, pressing her face to the rock hardness of his chest. Her arm was draped over his lean ribs and she paused to murmur. "Thank you," she whispered, grateful for his sacrifice. Already she felt groggy, as if she were floating away on a thick cloud. Her eyes felt heavy, and Simon was warm and smooth and wonderfully masculine. Gradually she could feel the tension drain out of him. After an exaggerated moment, he released a long, slow breath and curved an arm over her.

"I love you," Simon whispered sleepily as his hand roamed down her back in long soothing strokes.

His voice sounded far away. "I know," she murmured back and shifted her head so she could lightly kiss his jaw.

"Be good, understand?"

"Yes."

Neither spoke again and Angie drifted into a deep slumber, content to be in his arms.

Sometime during the morning, Angie's sleep became filled with resplendent, color-filled dreams that were vivid with detail. Pleasant dreams of when she was young and her mother was alive. Clay was handsome and happy, singing her his songs, and loving her mother with everything that was in him to love. Their trio was on a picnic by a clear, blue lake. The sun was shining and the birds sang merrily from the flowering trees. Clay and her mother and Angie were in a long wooden canoe on the crystal-clear water. Clay had brought along his guitar and was serenading them with the silly jingles he loved to create. Angie clapped her hands with delight and doubled over with laughter. When she straightened, her mother was gone and Clay sat across from her, old and gray-haired and in terrible pain. His hand was clenching his stomach and he looked at her in such agony that Angie cried out with shock. Clay begged her to get him to the hospital and Angie reached for the paddle—only it was missing. If she didn't hurry, Clay would die.

Frantic, Angie cried out again, her voice piercing the still room. Weeping and thrashing about, she knocked aside the blankets and bolted upright.

"Angie." The voice was low and frenzied and Angie opened her eyes to find Simon standing above her.

"Oh, Simon." Her breath came in deep, uneven gasps. "I had a horrible nightmare." Blindly she reached for him, seeking his comfort. Simon was her closest friend, her most trusted love. Vaguely she recalled that he had been in bed with her, but now it was obvious that he had come from the living room.

"It was a dream." He bent over her, his hands folding around her back.

Angie's arms tightened as she clung to him. "Hold me, please hold me." She whispered the words against his throat as her hands clenched at him with fear and anguish.

Simon braced a knee on the edge of the mattress and pulled aside the blankets as he came onto the bed and lay beside her. Angie's arms remained locked around his neck as the full length of his hard body joined her.

"Hold me, hold me," she repeated again and again.

Simon did as she asked with a tenderness and love she had known from no other. His large male hands stroked her hair, her shoulders and her back. Angie buried her face in the hollow of his throat and drew in deep, shaking breaths as she closed her eyes. He didn't try to soothe her with words, but simply held her, his hands caressing her.

Gradually the fear subsided and in its place came another emotion so strong, so powerful that her senses clamored with the intensity. Her grip relaxed and the muscles under her exploring fingers flexed powerfully. This was Simon holding her so tenderly. Her husband of twelve years.

As if aware of what was happening to her thoughts, Simon's hands stilled and he tossed back his head. "Angie?" His voice was filled with question.

She answered by kissing the salty-tasting skin at his throat, darting her tongue in and out in a provocative action.

"Angie," he pleaded hoarsely, "are you sure?"

In response, she kissed his Adam's apple, her tongue teasing and challenging him as it explored the throbbing pulse point on his neck.

"Angie, dear God."

"Love me, Simon. Please, oh please, love me."

Angie heard the sharply indrawn breath and opened her eyes to stare into the stormy, doubt-filled gray ones looking down on her.

Her hands slid over his shoulders and back again as their eyes continued to drink in each other. One palm slid down over his chest, and then lower, to the muscle-hard belly. "I want you," she whispered.

Simon groaned and positioned his hard body over hers. His breath was heavy, coming in deep pants as if he'd recently finished working out. He continued to hold her as he gradually lowered his mouth to hers, feasting on the sweetness of her lips with unhurried ease. He kissed her again and again until her mind was lost, incapable of any function beyond feeling the incredible sensations Simon awoke within her.

Leisurely, their tongues met with unhurried ease. Their movements soon took on a warring quality. They dueled, waged battle, caressed and touched, as a sweet fire swept through them.

Simon's hands were unsteady as he pulled the nylon gown over her head in an urgent movement. Tossing it carelessly aside, he reached for her again, his hands cupping the soft mounds of her breasts. He buried his face in their fullness, caressing her nipples with his tongue until they stood proud and regal before him.

"Simon," she moaned, her fingers digging into his hair as she arched her back to the exquisite sensations burning through her.

His lips found hers and she kissed him back greedily. Simon's fingers worked at removing the last barrier of his clothing that separated them. Free of the restricting material, he laid her back against the pillow and parted her thighs. Angie gripped his shoulders as he thrust into the enveloping warmth of her body. Together they moaned at the intense pleasure. Simon went still, his eyes squeezed shut, his teeth bared.

Gradually he began to move in a slow, easy rhythm until Angie thought she would die from the joyous rapture. Her body moved with his, eagerly meet-ing each relentless thrust. His mouth found hers in an unending kiss that soon became a harsh groan of pleasure.

Mindless of anything but the taste and feel of Simon, Angie dug long nails into his shoulder blades. The pleasure that had been denied her for twelve years burst forth gloriously within her and sent her swirling to the heights of heaven. She gave a small whimper and clenched his neck, kissing him again and again as the tears slid down her cheek.

Simon gave one final thrust, groaned and went still. Panting, he brushed the hair from her face and kissed her, tasting the salt of her tears.

"Angie, my sweet Angie, I'll love you on my dying day."

Her hands framed his face and she kissed him, her mouth slanting over his. "Simon," she whispered, poignantly moved by his lovemaking. "It's even better than I remember." She sniffled, smiling up at him. Lazily, his thumb wiped the moisture from her face.

"Yes," he agreed. He didn't move, kissing her again and again. "Am I too heavy for you?"

"Never." She closed her eyes, drinking in the warmth of his body sprawled over hers. "Don't leave me again."

"I won't," he murmured, close to her ear. "Never again."

Angie didn't know how or when it happened, but she fell into a deep slumber. She stirred once and felt the dead weight of Simon's arm over her waist. He was cuddling her, spoon fashion, in the narrow bed. The sound and feel of his even breathing assured her he was asleep. She nestled closer within his arms and returned to a contented, blissful sleep.

When she woke again it was to the warm sensation of someone kissing her earlobe.

Caught in the delicious sensations that shot through her, Angie rolled onto her back. "What time is it?" she asked, not bothering to open her eyes.

"Almost dinnertime."

Her eyes flew open. "That late?" She sat up, pulling the sheet with her. "I've got to . . ."

"I've already called the hospital. Your father is showing definite signs of improvement. He's not out of the woods yet, but he's in better shape than last night at this time," he told her, sitting beside her, fully dressed. His hands were positioned on the delicate slope of her shoulders and his gaze was filled with fierce tenderness.

It didn't seem possible that it was less than twenty-four hours ago that she had been sitting in a doctor's office with Clay.

"Are you hungry?" Simon questioned.

She smiled at him with all the love stored in her heart these past years. "Starved."

"Good. I took the liberty of snooping through your kitchen and fixing us something to eat."

Angie leaned against the headboard and stretched her arms out in a long yawn. "I feel wonderful."

Simon leaned forward and kissed her lightly. "You cried."

Self-conscious, Angie lowered her gaze. "I always did."

"I know," he said in a husky, low voice. "Angie . . ." He paused. "There hasn't been anyone else, has there." It was more a statement than question.

"No. I couldn't."

"Oh, Lord." He gathered her in his arms and buried his face in her throat. "I don't deserve you."

"I love you."

"I'm going to spend the rest of my life letting you know how much."

"Do you honestly think that'll be long enough," she teased.

Clay's eyes were closed when Angie moved into the hospital room an hour and a half later. The nurse standing at his bedside glanced up as Angie entered the room.

"He's been comfortable," the woman whispered, answering Angie's question before she could ask it. "He's showing signs of improvement."

Angie felt a rush of intense gratitude flow through her. "Good."

The nurse left a few minutes later, after charting her findings. Angie pulled out a chair and sat, taking Clay's hand between hers.

"Hi, Dad," she said softly. "Simon and I are back."

Simon stepped forward and placed a hand on Angie's shoulder. "I don't think he can hear you."

She turned around and smiled up at him warmly.

"Maybe not, but I feel better talking to him."

Simon located a chair and scooted it beside Angie's. "How is Clay going to feel about us?"

"I . . . I don't know." Some of her happiness dimmed. "Once I talk to him and explain how much I love you, then he'll come around."

"He's hated me for a lot of years."

"Simon, Clay doesn't hate you."

His hand squeezed her shoulder. "That's something we'll find out soon enough."

"Yes, I guess we will."

They sat, both caught in their doubts for a long half hour.

"Clay never says your name," Angie murmured. "He calls you 'that rich boy' or 'the Canfield boy.' He'll be surprised when he sees you to note that you're far from a lad."

Simon's soft chuckle was interrupted by a low strangling sound. At first Angie didn't hear it. Only when the amusement drained from Simon's eyes did Angie pick up on the soft sound. Standing, she stood over her father. "Daddy?"

"Angelcake." His voice was incredibly weak.

"How do you feel?"

"Like hell . . . should be dead."

"No," she protested.

Quietly, Simon stood and moved to the back of the room, out of Clay's line of vision.

"You did wonderfully well," she continued.

Clay scoffed at her with a small mocking sound. "Do the doctors expect me to kick the bucket?"

"No one's given up on you yet," Angie murmured softly and brushed the hair from his temple. "Least of all me."

"I may prove you right yet."

"Good."

Clay closed his eyes. The effort of keeping them open this short length of time had apparently drained him of all strength.

"Go back to sleep."

"I dreamed . . ."

"Shhh." She placed a finger over his lips. "We'll talk later."

Within minutes, Clay returned to a peaceful slumber. Angie tossed a triumphant glance to

Simon, her heart soaring. Her greatest fear had been that Clay would never wake up.

A jubilant sensation filled her breast. "He's going to be all right," she announced confidently, holding her hand out to Simon. "I can feel it in my bones."

Simon's arms slipped around her waist and he held her close. "I don't doubt that Clay Robinson will be seeing his grandchildren."

Angie and Simon left the hospital after visiting hours. Night was settling like a restless cloud over the land. The sky was dark and threatening, promising an imminent rainfall.

Simon followed Angie into her apartment.

"Angie." His voice was a husky caress. "Come here, love."

Obediently she walked into his embrace, sliding her arms around his waist and tilting her head back to smile at him. "You wanted something?" she teased.

"If only you knew."

"I think I do." She undid the first button of his shirt.

"Just what do you have in mind?" he asked with mock surprise.

"Let me show you, Mr. Canfield." The second button followed. She smiled a little and arched a suggestive brow. When the shirt was unfastened, she eased it from his shoulders and let it drop to the floor.

Hesitant at first, she reached out a hand and touched him, trailing her fingertips over the hard muscles of his naked torso. Simon closed his eyes and grinned. Angie's exploring hands paused at his belt buckle.

"You aren't going to stop now, are you?" he challenged.

"No." Her voice was shallow and low. Her hands resumed their task, and she stopped breathing completely. "Simon," she whispered, a little afraid. In their lovemaking he had always been the initiator.

Apparently understanding her hesitancy, he opened his eyes and kissed her lightly. "It's my turn now." He captured her hand and kissed her fingertips.

Seconds later her cotton blouse slid soundlessly to the floor and was soon followed by her slacks, so that she stood before him in only her bra and bikini panties.

"Oh, Angie," he moaned. "You are so beautiful."

She bowed her head and her dark hair fell forward, wreathing her face.

"What's wrong?" He raised her eyes to his. "You don't believe me?"

She couldn't answer him with words. Instead she stood on her tiptoes and kissed him. "Thank you," she whispered reverently. "Thank you for loving me."

"Oh, Angie." He picked her up and carried her into the bedroom, stopping every few steps to press a thick, seductive kiss to her eager mouth.

He laid her on the unmade bed, his mouth feasting on hers while his hands fumbled with the tiny hook of her bra. Once it was free, he tugged it from her arms. His attention wandered from her mouth to the taut nipples. His hot, moist breath seemed to scorch her breasts and he teased the tight buds with his teeth. Angie gasped as his hand stroked downward to her navel and across her abdomen to the elastic waistband of her lace panties. Lost in a mindless whirl of anticipation, Angie lifted her hips as he dragged her underwear down her legs. Unconcerned, she kicked them free.

Standing, Simon removed his clothes and threw them aside. Joining her on the bed once again, he was upon her, crushing her with his weight and urgency.

"Oh, love," he breathed. "I want you so much."

Moaning, she parted her legs in invitation. With a low growl, Simon thrust into her, his maleness impaling her softness as he cried out her name.

Long afterward, Angie lay in his arms, her head cradled in the crook of his arm. Lazily her fingers toyed with the short, dark hair that grew at his navel. Words weren't necessary. They were completely and utterly content. The living room light dispersed its golden shadow into the bedroom, and when Angie lifted her head she was surprised to note that Simon was asleep.

Easing herself from his embrace, she kissed him lightly on the forehead and reached for her robe, wrapping it around her nakedness. As ideal as their few moments together had been, there were still many roads they had yet to traverse. Gazing down at him, Angie's heart swelled with love. Together, she knew they would cross any bridge that was necessary. As long as they were together, nothing else mattered.

Angie was in the kitchen putting on coffee when the doorbell rang. Her hand froze and she looked frantically toward the bedroom. There was only one person who would visit this late. Dread settled over her as she toyed with the idea of ignoring the bell. But Glenn would only ring again and wake Simon. That thought caused her to hurry across the room and open the door.

"Angie." Glenn stepped past her into the room. "Where the hell have you been? I've been trying to get you for the past two days." He paused as if taking in her appearance for the first time. "I didn't get you out of bed, did I?" He checked his watch. "It's barely ten."

"Clay's in the hospital."

Glenn raked his hand through his hair. "I feared as much. What was wrong and for God's sake why didn't you call me?"

"I . . ." She struggled for the right words. She didn't want to hurt Glenn.

"Angie?" Simon staggered into the room, his hair in disarray. His hastily donned pants left little to conjecture as to his whereabouts. He stopped cold and straightened when he caught sight of Glenn. The two men eyed each other with shocked disbelief.

≈ Eleven ≈

Glenn's mouth twisted up at one corner as he regarded Angie with shock and embarrassment. "How long has this been going on?"

"Glenn, please, I'm so sorry . . ." Angie's eyes pleaded with him.

"Angie's been under a lot of stress," Simon intervened, as he stepped into the room.

Angie glanced at Simon and murmured, "Let me have a few minutes alone with Glenn."

His nod was filled with understanding. He returned to the bedroom and was back a minute later fully dressed. He paused by the front door, his eyes warming her as he murmured that he'd be back in fifteen minutes. The door made a clicking sound as it closed.

She smiled her appreciation and turned back to Glenn. His thick brows were bunched together to form a single intense line. His eyes were so cold and angry they looked as if they had frosted over. The clenched jaw was white and a muscle twitched warningly. Angie had never seen Glenn like this.

"Glenn," she began haltingly, "I can't tell you how sorry I am that you found out about Simon and me this way."

"Tell me one thing," he ground out savagely.

"How long have you been sleeping with him?"

Angie struggled to keep her voice calm, but her eyes pleaded with him for understanding. "Today was the first time . . . I would have let you know only . . ."

"Only what, Angie? Only you thought you might be able to hold on to me a while longer, is that it?"

"No," she wailed loudly.

"I've always been honest with you, Angie. But I was a fool to expect that same kind of integrity from you."

"Glenn," she begged, "it's not like that."

"Then what was it like? You made a fool out of me. Couldn't you have had the common decency to let me know about Clay? At least then I wouldn't have worried and shown up here like an idiot."

She struggled to find the words. "You have been the most wonderful, patient man in the world."

"I'm not St. Thomas Aquinas," he barked. "Don't try to pin those saintly virtues on me. I loved you. I wanted you to be my wife. But most of all I respected and trusted you."

"I know what this must look like—"

"It looks like exactly what it is: a sordid affair with an old lover."

"No." Angie recognized that Glenn was lashing out at her with his pain, but she couldn't allow him to distort the love she shared with Simon. "I won't have you talk to me like that. I've loved Simon all my life. You knew as well as I did that . . . that if I'd married you I could never have given you the love you deserved."

Glenn's reply was a low, mocking snort. "Do you want me to give you a medal because you gave Simon the love *he* deserved?"

"Dear God, Glenn, you've twisted everything."

"I don't know," he argued, "it seems that for the first time in six months, I'm finally seeing everything clearly. You used me to get Simon back. That's what you really wanted—your old lover."

Angie could see that arguing was useless. "You have been extremely patient and dear. I'm so sorry everything's turned out like this, but when . . . when Clay became deathly ill I knew I couldn't face losing him without Simon. He was the one I reached out to."

Glenn grimaced and his clenched jaw tightened all the more.

"I wouldn't want to hurt you for the world. I can't tell you how sorry I am."

"Sorry. You're sorry?" He glared at her explosively.

"I owe you so much. It pains me to do this to you."

"I was the fool," Glenn barked. "A hundred times I could have had you. We should have been married weeks ago and you wouldn't have any choice but to stay with me."

His words were cruel and mocking and with every minute he looked more enraged.

"I don't think there's any way to make this up to you. But I want you to know there will always be a special place in my heart for you."

"You used me."

Angie couldn't deny it. "Please try to forget me, Glenn, and forgive me if you can. A thousand women would count themselves lucky to be loved by you."

"But you're not one of them."

Her gaze dropped to the floor. "I'm sorry . . . so sorry."

"Don't waste that emotion on me." The air between them was as tight as a hunter's bow stretched to its limits, ready to spring. "I can see there's no need to waste my time here. Enjoy your lover, Angie."

She kept her eyes shut until after the door was viciously closed. The harsh sound reverberated around the room.

A few minutes later, Simon knocked lightly against the front door. Angie hurried across the room to let him in. Instinctively she reached for him. He folded her to his embrace, his hands running soothingly down her back.

Gratefully she accepted his comfort, pleased that he had given her this time alone with Glenn.

It hadn't been easy for him, she'd known that by the troubled look in his eye.

"What did he say?" Simon asked.

She shook her head hard. "It isn't important."

"He was hurt and angry."

"I wish I could have spared him the pain of finding us like this. I blame myself for that. I should have called him."

"He'll recover," Simon said confidently.

"I hope so," she whispered, tightening her grip. "Dear Lord, I hope so."

They slept in each other's arms, content just to cuddle close. It surprised Angie that after all the years of sleeping alone her body would adjust so easily to sharing a bed. Somehow she knew it wouldn't have been that way with another man. Only Simon.

She woke to find him grinning at her beguilingly. "Morning," he whispered and kissed her warmly.

Angie looped her arms around his neck and smiled into his eyes. "I could get used to waking up next to you."

"You'd better. I don't plan to sleep without you."

"Good." Her index finger wove around his curly chest hairs. "Have I told you lately how much I love you?"

"No." Simon's voice was deep and resonant.

"Yes, I have." She giggled. "You simply weren't listening."

"Hmm, I was listening," he said and buried his face in the rounding slope of her shoulder to tease her unmercifully with small, biting kisses. "But I'm a man of action. Shall I demonstrate just how much I love you?"

"Oh, yes," she whispered, her leg sliding provocatively up and down his. "But I feel I should warn you, it may take a lifetime to prove it to me properly."

"You drive a hard bargain, Angie Canfield," he growled before hungrily lowering his mouth to claim hers.

The morning was half spent before they ever left the bedroom.

After a leisurely brunch Angie dressed and prepared herself for a visit to the hospital.

"You've gotten quiet all of a sudden." Simon stood behind her, his hands cupping her shoulders as she rinsed off the breakfast dishes. "Are you worried about your father?"

Angie had phoned the hospital twice and each time received an encouraging report. "No," she whispered unconvincingly.

"You're frightened of what he's going to say about us, aren't you, love?"

"I'm afraid it's all going to happen again." She turned around and gripped his waist, pressing her cheek to his chest. She was comforted by the even, reassuring sound of his heartbeat. "Dad hates Groves Point . . ."

"And the Canfields," Simon added.

"Yes."

"But he's forgetting something important. Something that we'll need to remind him today, if necessary. You, Angie, are a Canfield. You have been for twelve years."

"But, Simon . . ." she argued and lifted her head to meet his gaze.

He pressed a finger to her lips, silencing her. "Today we'll make it clear that we have no intention of ever being separated again."

"But he's ill."

"Good," Simon argued, "there won't be much fight in him. He'll simply have to accept what we say."

Angie didn't feel any of the confidence Simon apparently did when they drove to the hospital. She hesitated outside Clay's room. "Maybe it would be better if I talked to him first," she suggested, her eyes seeking his approval.

Simon hesitated. "You're sure you don't want me with you?"

She answered him with a short nod, laid her open palms on his hard chest and kissed him briefly on the lips.

Clay was awake when Angie entered the room. He didn't make an effort to greet her. From the disapproving look in his eyes, Angie wondered if Glenn had come to Clay. As quickly as the thought came, Angie rejected it. Glenn would never do anything so petty. Clay looked so incredibly pale that her steps faltered. The hospital had assured her that her father was out of immediate danger, but she knew that the road to a complete recovery would be long and difficult.

"Hi, Dad." She leaned over and brushed her lips to his forehead.

"What took you so long? I've been waiting for you all morning. The least you could do is visit a dying man who happens to be your only living relative."

Feelings of guilt immediately assailed her. "I . . . woke late. When I called the hospital they said you were resting comfortably."

"Ha! That just goes to show you what they know."

"I'm here now." She clenched his hand in hers and held it close to her heart. "How are you feeling?"

"How in the hell do you expect me to feel? The pain would have killed most men. I nearly died. Do you think those doctors were gentle with that knife?"

"No . . . you suffered terribly."

"It ain't much better now."

Angie sighed miserably. This wasn't going well. Clay was like a demanding, unreasonable child. She lowered her gaze to the hospital bed and the white sheets. "I have something to tell you." Her voice nearly failed her and her resolve wasn't much better. If Simon hadn't been standing on the other side of the door, Angie wouldn't have had the courage to continue. "When you were so deathly ill and I didn't know if you were going to live or die, I was so afraid. I was terrified of losing you."

Clay patted her hand impatiently. "You nearly did lose me. That's why I can't understand the reason it took you so long to get to the hospital." He looked at her empty hands. "And the least you could do is bring me the newspaper."

Angie felt like gritting her teeth. "Clay, let me finish. I . . . I thought you were going to die and I reached out to someone I've loved forever . . . someone I knew would comfort me." She swallowed against the tightness forming in her throat. "I called Simon Canfield." Not waiting for a reaction she quickly moved to the door and stepped outside the room and took Simon's hand. He smiled encouragingly at her and squeezed her fingers.

By the time they entered the room, Clay had half risen from the bed, lifting himself up on one elbow. His face was contorted with rage and fury. "Get out," he hissed. "I won't have Canfield scum in my room."

"Clay," Angie cried.

"And you get with him. If you don't know any better than to bring him here when I'm dying then you ain't no daughter to me."

The color drained from Angie's face. "Don't say that."

"I'll say that and more." He fumbled with the button to summon the nurse and fell limply against the pillow, his face twisted with pain. "Get out."

"Maybe you have reason to hate me," Simon said, fighting to control his temper. "But I love Angie and I won't allow you to come between us, old man. So understand that here and now."

The nurse with the crisp white uniform entered the room. "Get them out of here." Clay pointed a finger accusingly at Simon and Angie. "Leave me to die in peace." His voice shook, he was so weak. The pale features were filled with angry color as he glared accusingly at Simon.

The nurse's face was grim as she turned to Angie. "Maybe it would be best if you came back another time."

Angie blinked back the scalding tears that threatened to spill.

"Just get one thing clear," Simon said in a low, hard voice. "I'm marrying your daughter and nothing on God's good earth is going to prevent that."

Clay lay on his back and stared at the ceiling, his features void of expression. "I ain't got a daughter."

"Daddy," Angie cried.

"Leave him to sulk," Simon whispered, gripping her elbow.

The nurse followed them out of the room, closing the door behind her. She hesitated and cleared her throat. "I don't want to become involved in family squabbles, but I feel you should understand that at this point your father's condition is extremely delicate. It would be best if you didn't do or say anything to upset him. If coming here is going to provoke him, then I suggest you stay away."

"But . . ." Angie couldn't bear the thought of having Clay step back from the brink of death only to lose him to stubborn pride.

"Anyone of the staff would be happy to report his condition to you," the older woman continued.

"You don't think I should come at all?" Angie was aghast at the thought.

"Not if it's going to drain his strength. Your father is going to need all the fight he can muster just to recover properly."

"Come on, Angie." The pressure of Simon's hand at Angie's elbow increased. "Let's get out of here."

She nodded and smiled her appreciation to the nurse who had spoken so freely. On the ride back to her apartment, Angie didn't say a word, her thoughts dragging her spirits lower and lower with every mile.

Simon pulled into her parking lot and turned

off the engine. For a long minute they didn't move. "What are you going to do?" he asked finally.

"What can I do?" she choked and covered her face with her hands. "Simon, he's my father."

"I'm your husband."

Angie felt as if the two men were waging a battle over her. Each was pulling on an arm, driving a wedge between Angie the daughter and Angie the woman, placing her in an impossible position.

Simon looped an arm around her shoulders and breathed into her hair. His voice was a gentle whisper close to her ear. "Let's go inside. We can talk there."

They made two cups of strong coffee and sat next to each other on the sofa. Simon's shoulder supported Angie's head as they became lost in the tangled web of their disturbed thoughts.

"With my own father so ill, I can appreciate your position," Simon began hesitantly. "The best solution would be for us to separate ourselves from family altogether. I could leave Groves Point and you could leave Charleston and we'd start a new life."

"We can't do that," Angie protested.

"I know, love." Wearily, he leaned his head back and let his eyes slip closed. "With my father sick, it'd be impossible for me to leave Groves Point."

"And Clay needs me in the same way."

"If you think I'm going to suggest the noble thing, you're wrong," he said quietly. His hand gripped her in a punishing hold. He'd endured too many miserable years without Angie. A hot anger surged through him at the thought of facing more of the same. He couldn't part with her when he'd come this close.

"What are we going to do?" Angie whispered, close to tears.

"About the only thing we can do for now. Wait. When Clay is back on his feet, we'll face him again. Only next time we won't back down. Agreed?"

Angie didn't hesitate. "Agreed."

Simon returned to Groves Point three days later when he could no longer ignore the commitments awaiting him. Clay Robinson was released from the hospital sixteen days after being admitted. Angie had visited him daily. At first he refused to speak to her. That was fine, she did most of the talking, chatting with him about little things that went on at the flower shop. She brought him the afternoon edition of the newspaper, his mail and a daily supply of fresh-cut flowers. After a day or two Clay started asking her about Simon. Angie ignored his questions.

"You aren't seeing him, are you?" Clay had demanded.

Angie opened the blind and stared into the sun. "I can't ever remember a more glorious after-noon. The sun is brilliant."

After two or three days of that type of response, Clay quit asking.

Because his condition remained weak and he would need someone to care for him, Angie drove her father to her apartment when he was released from the hospital. "You're to stay here until you're completely well, understand?" She didn't expect much of an argument. Clay knew a good thing when he saw it.

The situation wasn't ideal, but it soothed Angie's conscience.

With Clay at the apartment, Simon, who phoned daily, was forced to contact Angie at Clay Pots. Their conversations were often short as she was interrupted by customers and the usual hectic activity of running a flower shop.

"Simon." She drank in the sound of his voice after one particularly bad morning. "I'm so glad to hear your voice."

"How's Clay?"

"Demanding."

"In other words he's running you ragged."

"Nothing seems to satisfy him," came her trembling reply. "Yesterday he called me three times with different requests. He wanted me to pick up his mail, which I do every night anyway. Then he didn't like what I'd planned to cook for his dinner and wanted me to shop at the grocery store and pick up something that wasn't on his diet. I don't know why he bothered to ask. He knew I wouldn't."

"Angie, this can't go on much longer."

"I know," she agreed with an exaggerated sigh. "He's playing the deathbed recovery to the hilt. He makes it sound as if each request is his last."

"If I got hold of him it would be."

A slow smile touched her tired eyes. "Simon, just let me complain. I need someone to sympathize with me."

"I'm willing to comfort you as well." His voice went low and suggestive.

"Are you now?"

"Eager even."

Angie giggled. "I bet you're not half as eager as me."

"Oh, Lord, Angie, don't say things like that. Three hundred miles never seemed so far. I'm dying for you."

"It shouldn't be much longer," she promised. "Clay's going to the doctor tomorrow afternoon. I'll ask about having him move back to his own place. As much as I love my father, he's driving me crazy."

"Another minute without you is too long," Simon argued. "I'm coming this weekend."

"Simon." She breathed his name, pushing the

237

hair back from her forehead with one hand. "Do you think you should?"

"I'll go crazy if I don't."

"Me too," she admitted.

"You are going to marry me, aren't you?"

Her smile was filled with contentment. "I've been your wife in my heart for twelve years. I'd say it was time we made it legal."

"More than time."

Donna glanced to the back of the shop and Angie straightened. "I've got to go."

"Me too."

But neither hung up. "Bye, love."

"I love you, Simon Canfield."

"You better, I'm counting on collecting on that promise this weekend."

Saturday morning, after being assured by the doctor that Clay would be with her for another two weeks and perhaps longer, Angie was as nervous as a teenager about Simon's visit. Simon's commuter plane was due to arrive shortly after noon. From the airport he was checking into a hotel, where she was meeting him for lunch.

"What's the matter with you this morning?" Clay snapped. "You're as jumpy as water on a hot griddle."

"Sorry."

"You should be sorry to leave a sick man on a Saturday."

"That can't be helped," she said and swallowed down the guilt.

"Where did you say you was going?"

"To a meeting."

"You're dressed up mighty pretty for a simple meetin'."

"This one is with someone important."

Clay snorted. "You just remember what that fancy doctor said. I ain't out of the woods yet. I could have a relapse any day."

"You're getting stronger by the minute," she countered. Checking her watch, Angie brought Clay the television guide and kissed him briefly on the cheek. Dutifully, she tucked the blanket around his waist.

"What time will you be back?"

"I . . . don't know."

"The least you can do is give me a phone number where I can reach you in case something terrible happens while you leave me."

Angie froze, making a pretense of checking the insides of her purse. "That could be difficult, I'll have to call you."

"The person you should be calling is Glenn."

Glenn's name had been mentioned at least five times every day. "How come he ain't been around lately? I would have thought Glenn would stop by to see me. It's the least my future son-in-law could do." He paused and Angie could feel the heat of his gaze as he studied her.

Angie decided the best thing to do was ignore him. "Bye, Clay." The minute the door was closed, Angie released a pent-up breath and relaxed. This was worse than anything she'd endured in her secret meetings with Simon the summer they were seventeen.

The drive seemed to take forever, Angie was anxious to get to him. She was afraid of wasting a single minute, afraid Clay would demand an accounting of her afternoon.

Simon was waiting for her in the hotel lobby. Their eyes met from across the width of the room. At the intense emotion shining from his deep, gray ones, Angie paused. He seemed to be digesting everything about her as if he couldn't deter-mine if she was illusion or reality.

The tension eased from Angie and she offered him a trembling smile of happiness. They met halfway into the room.

"Hi," she whispered, as their eyes drank in the sight of each other.

"You are so beautiful." He stopped himself from taking her in his arms and kissing her in front of a lobby full of people. Impatiently he glanced around. "Are you hungry?"

Shyly, Angie lowered her lashes. "Only for you."

"Room service?" he asked with a chuckle, tucking her hand in the crook of his arm.

"I think we'd better."

The minute they were inside Simon's suite, he

took her in his arms and kissed her with a hunger that had been building inside of him for three interminable weeks. They undressed each other with trembling, eager hands, pausing only long enough to kiss. Their bodies were on fire for each other, their mouths clinging, twisting, yearning. Their hands paused only to explore with awe and promise. When they were both completely nude, Simon's head drew back to look into her dark eyes. His thumbs lovingly brushed the high arch of her cheekbones.

"Oh, my sweet love." He dropped his forehead against hers. "I love you so much I think I'd die without you now."

"I'll always be yours," she whispered emotionally, then surrendered to the exquisite agony he inflicted upon her with his hands and mouth. Angie thought she would die from the sweet torture before he carried her to the bed. He took her then with a savage tenderness that was unlike anything she had ever known.

When they had finished, Simon drew her into his arms and kissed the trail of tears that ran down her cheek. Nestled in his embrace, she laid her cheek upon his chest and breathed in even, contented breaths, thinking that nothing this side of heaven could be more wonderful than being loved by Simon.

"Are you asleep?" he whispered after a long moment.

"I don't want to waste a moment of our time together by sleeping." Each second was precious. Angie didn't know how long it would be before she could see him again.

"In some ways I think I'm going crazy. I'm still warm and content from loving you and already I'm worried about how soon it'll be before I can have you again."

She smiled and kissed his neck, letting her tongue tease his Adam's apple. "Any time, Mr. Bank President."

His arms tightened around her. "Angie, I've thought of a way to bridge the gap between our parents."

He sounded so serious that she lifted her head and turned onto her side, supporting her head with the palm of her hand. "You must be more of a genius than I give you credit for."

"A baby," he whispered reverently, placing a hand on her trim stomach. "The best thing that could happen to us is to get you pregnant as soon as possible."

Angie closed her eyes to the tenderness in his voice.

"My mother would give anything for a grand-child. I can think of nothing better to make us acceptable to the other's parents."

Angie recalled Clay's words about wanting to bounce a "grandbaby" on his knee. "Jeffrey Simon Canfield," she responded dreamily.

"Or Carolyn Angela Canfield." His hand traveled from her smooth stomach to capture her breast. "Only I think we should think about getting this marriage made legal and the sooner the better."

Tears of happiness brimmed on Angie's eyelashes. "Yes," she said and gave him a watery smile, "I think we should."

"Next weekend?"

Angie shook her head. "I don't ever expect Clay to give me his whole-hearted approval, but I'd rather wait until he's at least well enough to be on his own."

Simon's hand caressed her shoulders. "As soon as possible, though."

"Yes," she agreed.

Long after Angie had left, Simon lay staring at the tiled hotel ceiling. A feeling of dread he couldn't shake settled over him. He didn't usually have premonitions, but the fear continued to grow in his chest until he couldn't bear to stay still. Jerking to a sitting position, he sat on the edge of the mattress and buried his face in his hands. Angie was so close to being his. He could think of no reason that this fear should assail him now. She loved him more than he dared believe, more than he deserved. They had talked of making their marriage legal and starting a family. There were twelve years of wasted time to make up. Years of love and laughter.

He glanced at the phone, more than half-tempted to call her. These past few weeks he had lived for those few minutes each day when they spoke. It was never enough time.

The irony of their situation caused a frown to mar his brow. Twelve years ago, his family had stood in their way. They'd been forced to meet secretly then. They had been married twelve years and the first time he'd spent the night with Angie had been when Clay was in the hospital. Now they were compelled into that same kind of clandestine meeting, only it was her father who was keeping them apart. Their relationship, he thought pensively, was only a sad reflection of yesterday.

Angie let herself into the apartment and painted a smile on her face. Her heart was heavy. In some ways it would have been easier not to have seen Simon. It hurt so much to say good-bye.

"How are you feeling, Dad?"

"I thought you were going to call?" He didn't take his eyes from the television.

"I'm sorry, I forgot." Angie knew immediately that she'd said the wrong thing.

Angrily, Clay tossed the television guide to the floor. "Your own father is near death and you run off to some all-important meeting and completely forget about him."

"I didn't mean it that way." She flushed guiltily.

"It'd serve you right if I was to up and die."

"Good grief, I was only gone three hours."

"And ten minutes. I'm bored. Did you bring me my mail? I wasn't hungry at lunchtime, but I could eat something now. You can bring it in to me."

Gritting her teeth, Angie stepped into the kitchen and took the lunch she'd made for him earlier out of the refrigerator. She carried it out to him on a tray. "Do you want anything else?"

He ignored the question. "The way you snuck off like that one would think you were hurrying to meet a lover."

Angie's step faltered, causing her to nearly drop the lunch tray. "Stop being so dramatic," she chastised in her sternest voice. She set the lunch on the coffee table and straightened.

"That's exactly what you was doing, wasn't it?"

Angie returned to the kitchen, her composure rapidly disintegrating. "The subject isn't open for discussion."

"You're a fool, girl."

"And you're interfering in my life."

Clay pushed the tray aside, disinterested. "Tell me somethin'. What makes you think that those highfalutin' Canfield folks is going to want you any more the second time than they did the first.

Can you see Mrs. Canfield inviting you to the Garden Club. Not hardly."

"I'm not talking to you about it."

"Sure you're not, 'cause you can't answer me. Nothin's changed in twelve years that will make you more acceptable to those rich folks."

"Clay, you heard me. I refuse to discuss this with you."

"All these years I thought I was raising me a decent girl," he mumbled as he crossed his arms and leaned back against the pillows supporting his shoulders. "You ain't no better than a common . . ." He hesitated, apparently thinking better of his choice of words. "You're making a big mistake, little girl. I'm begging you to reconsider having anything to do with the Canfields."

"Dad. Why do you have to do this to me? I love him. If Mom had come from a rich Atlanta family would you have loved her less? Would you have decided not to marry her?"

Clay's cheeks expanded until he looked as if he were about to explode. "I won't have you dragging the good name of your mother into this. You hear me, girl?"

"I hear you," Angie said, her voice coated with defeat.

≈ Twelve ≈

At five-thirty Angie closed up Clay Pots for the night. She had finished counting the money from the till when there was a knock at the bolted glass door. Glancing up from behind the counter she was shocked to see Glenn standing on the other side.

"Glenn," she murmured, turning the dead-bolt lock.

"Hello, Angie." He regarded her sheepishly. "I apologize for stopping by unexpectedly."

"Please come in." She resecured the lock. "Is something wrong?" He didn't look right. He was darker, tanner, as if he'd spent lots of time in the intervening weeks working outside. As always he was meticulously dressed in a three-piece business suit and silk tie. Glenn had always been a stickler for neatness.

"I've come to ask you to forgive me for the things I said the last time I saw you."

"My forgiveness," she gasped. "Oh, Glenn, don't make me cry." He was such a wonderful, dear man and she had hurt him immeasurably, and then *he* came to apologize.

"What I said that night was unforgivable."

"You were only reacting to your anger. I don't hold any of it against you. We've been good friends for a long time. I knew you didn't mean it."

"I've felt bad about it for weeks. In thinking it over, I realized that the only thing to do was to come back and tell you that I wish you and Simon every happiness. I'll always love you, Angie, but I know that you belong with Simon. The only thing I want is to be certain that my anger didn't hurt you in any way."

"It didn't. I understood."

"I thought you might, but I wanted to be sure." An uncomfortable silence followed. It was so good to see Glenn again; she had missed his friendship, especially now that Clay was recovering and being so difficult.

As if reading her mind, Glenn asked, "How's Clay?"

"On the mend. Why don't you stop by and visit him sometime? He's at my apartment and I know he'd love to see you. He's bored and out of sorts and would welcome the company."

"Would you?"

Angie lowered her gaze, ill at ease. She didn't want to give Glenn any reason to hope there was a chance they could get back together again.

"I didn't mean it that way," he amended. "I only wanted to make sure that you didn't mind if I came by."

"I wouldn't have asked you otherwise." Briefly her hand touched his in an assuring action.

"You don't look happy, Angie. What's wrong?"

How like Glenn to look past his own troubles to recognize and comfort her. "Clay has strong feelings about Simon and me. He doesn't want me to have anything to do with the Canfields, let alone marry Simon. There's a continual cold war waging between us that is wearing me down." It felt so good to talk to someone about Clay. Someone who would understand. Any mention of her difficulties with her father would have only added to Simon's problems. And he'd been having plenty of those lately.

"In other words he's constantly nipping at your heels."

Glenn had a way of describing it perfectly. "Yes."

The worst part was that Simon's father had died suddenly and Simon had been tied up in Groves Point for the past two weeks. Angie's heart had gone out to him in his grief, recalling her own overwhelming emotion when Clay had been close to death. Simon had explained that he'd known for several months that his father was extremely ill. The two had never been close and although he gave no outward sign of oppressive sadness, Angie knew that the death had affected him greatly. Many times in the past weeks she had wanted to be with him, to offer what comfort she could. Simon had assured her that he under-stood the reason she couldn't. He was fine. Just knowing that she loved him and wanted to be with him was enough for now. The demands on his time from his mother, settling his father's affairs and those of the bank had prevented him from coming to Charleston. But he would be there as soon as circumstances would allow. Angie lived for their daily telephone conversations.

For the funeral Angie had sent an elaborate floral arrangement, but Georgia Canfield hadn't acknowledged the gift. Angie comforted herself with the knowledge that it was too soon to expect a note of appreciation.

Only when Clay continued to harp on the differences between the two families, the Robinsons and "those rich folks in Groves Point," was it difficult to dismiss the doubts. Simon was sure that their love would construct all the bridges necessary. If not, fine. They didn't need anyone else, they had each other. Angie's confirming echo grew weaker every day. She needed Clay, and as much as she resented his intrusion into her life, he was her father. Clay had been her staunch supporter when she started in the flower business and now it was her turn to stand by him. Clay's unfailing belief in her had helped Angie at a time in her life that she'd needed it most. As far as he was concerned there wasn't a thing in this world that she couldn't do. Even though she'd bragged to Simon about Petal Pushers, Clay had often helped her. Some days he had spent more hours than she had, taking her assignments until Angie found her feet with Clay Pots. Unwittingly Clay had worked to repay the Canfields all those thousands. Although Simon might not readily agree, he relied on his mother, too. Especially now. In death Simon's father had healed the gap between mother and son. They shared an emotional bond and as the days passed it became all the more evident that Georgia Canfield needed Simon for moral and mental support during the difficult days.

"Maybe you'd like to come tonight," Angie suggested to Glenn. "Make it a surprise for Clay."

The handsome male features broke into a smile. "I'd like that. I'll follow you."

A couple of times Angie checked her rearview mirror on the way home. Glenn had been stopped at a yellow light at a major intersection so she was about three minutes ahead of him when she came through the door.

She greeted Clay with a warm smile and kissed his cheek. "How was your day?"

He grunted and threw back the blanket that covered his legs. "About as good as you can expect a man to feel who's been cooped up in a stuffy apartment for the last month of his life."

"But, Dad!" Her voice rose indignantly. "I've begged and pleaded with you to get some fresh air. It's not good for you to sit around all day and do nothing."

"You're just looking for a way to kill me off so you can marry that rich Canfield boy."

Angie's fingers curled around the leather strap of her purse as she battled down the rising irritation. Clay had been living with her for almost a month now and every day the atmosphere grew more strained.

"I've got a surprise for you."

"Don't want no surprises."

"I think you'll like this one," she said confidently.

The doorbell chimed and Clay's eyes flew to the front door. "Why don't you get that? The exercise will do you good." Not waiting for an argument, Angie disappeared into her bedroom where she changed into a cool pair of shorts and a sleeveless knit pullover. She paused and smiled when she heard Clay's happy exclamation of surprise.

Slipping her feet into sandals, she returned to the living room to discover Clay sitting on the sofa, his shoulders shaking with huge sobs. "She's going to marry him. I know it in my heart, and he'll ruin her for decent men just the way he did twelve years ago."

"Clay!" Angie gasped. She couldn't believe that her own father would talk about her this way.

"See what I mean," Clay said and leaned closer to Glenn. Tears ran unrestrained down his face. "Already he's turned her against me. You've got to do something." Clay's hands gripped Glenn's forearm as he regarded the younger man with pleading, sad eyes.

"If anyone's turned against anybody, it's you against me." To her horror, tears stung the back of her eyes.

"Angie." Glenn stood and crossed the room, taking her by the shoulders. "Listen, it's easy to see that you've worn yourself to a frazzle taking care of your father. Let me stay with him tonight. Go do some shopping or take in a movie. Anything. Just leave for a while and relax."

"But I've got to fix his dinner."

His finger lazily wiped a lone tear from her cheek. "I've cooked before."

"He's on a special diet."

"Clay knows what he can and can't eat. Now, don't you worry about it. Just go and enjoy yourself."

She placed her hand in his and squeezed it with all the appreciation in her heart. "Thank you."

She left without saying a word to Clay who sat regarding her mutinously. His eyes were slightly red as he glared at her angrily.

In the mood for a peaceful ride, Angie drove to Sullivan's Island and walked along the sandy beach for what seemed like hours. A gentle breeze ruffled her hair and the tangy scent of saltwater followed her as the waves crashed against the peaceful shore. Her thoughts weren't profound. She was too run-down, mentally and physically, to deal with any of the problems that plagued her. She didn't want to think about Clay or Simon or anyone. The beach had often offered her solace she couldn't find elsewhere. As if not to disappoint her, the sky turned a vibrant shade of pink and the warm sand welcomed her bare feet. Granules of the wet beach squished between her toes as she sat and stared out over the swelling rolling waters, at peace at last with her world.

It seemed ironic that the one to rescue her from another night of bickering with Clay would be Glenn, the man she had rejected. Intuitively, it seemed, Glenn had known when she was at her weakest point, struggling to maintain some semblance of sanity. Glenn Lambert was a rare man, she realized anew.

After a peace-filled hour, Angie located a pay phone and using her credit card called Groves Point.

"Yes." Simon's answer was abrupt and impatient as if he, too, was stretched to the limits with the demands and pressures made on him.

"Hello, Simon." It was so good to hear him that the effort to keep her voice steady was monumental.

"Angie." Her name was issued on a rush of air that sounded like a warm caress. "Is anything wrong?"

Nothing was right, but Simon didn't need to

hear that. He was under enough stress as it was. "No," she answered softly, "I just needed to hear the sound of your voice." She could almost feel the tension drain out of him as he began to speak.

"Where are you? I can hear a strange noise in the background."

"Landlubber," she teased affectionately, "don't you know the sound of the ocean when you hear it?"

"The ocean? Where are you?"

"You won't believe this."

"Knowing you, I'd believe anything," he said, chuckling.

"I'm on Sullivan Island. Here, listen." She opened the door to the small pay-phone cubicle and pointed the telephone receiver toward the beach. "What do you think?"

"I think I'm going to go crazy if I don't see you soon."

"This weekend?" she asked, trying to disguise how anxious she was.

Simon hesitated, his voice filled with angry frustration when he spoke. "Honey, I can't. There are a thousand things I have to do with Dad's estate."

"Don't worry, we've got the rest of our lives. Another week or two isn't going to matter." She tried desperately to hide her disappointment.

A long moment of silence stretched between them.

"How's Clay?" Simon asked finally.

Angie forced a light laugh. "Cantankerous as ever. He seems to be recovering, but he refuses to do any exercise." Angie had come to believe that he was purposely making himself an invalid to prevent her from marrying Simon. Only she wasn't going to allow him to do that. The next appointment with Clay's doctor was the following week. Once Clay was given a clean bill of health, she was moving him back to his own place so fast it'd make his head swim.

"How are you?" Simon asked next.

"Cantankerous as ever," she said with a light laugh. "I miss you, and I wish I was pregnant so Clay would insist that you make an honest woman of me and fall right into our plans."

Simon chuckled. "My thoughts toward you at the moment are completely dishonest. Oh Lord, Angie, I love you. I can hardly wait to show you how much."

"Believe me, I'm just as eager to prove my love." Where Angie had felt cold and tense before, she now felt warm, loved and utterly secure.

They talked for an hour of silly inanities and ones not so silly. It was the most time they'd had together since Simon's one-day visit to Charleston two weeks before.

Even when she replaced the receiver, Angie felt the warm glow of contentment that covered her with its serenity. Times were difficult for them now, but they would be better and soon. It was vital that she didn't look down at the mire she was standing in, but raise her line of vision to the long and happy life that stretched ahead of her with Simon.

Simon replaced the telephone receiver and twined his fingers behind his head, balancing his chair on two legs as he leaned against the kitchen wall. Without Angie these past two weeks, he would have been driven to the edge of insanity. He had known and accepted that his father was gravely ill, but his death had still caught Simon unprepared. He had heard that from others but hadn't recognized the truth until his own father had gone. Maybe if he hadn't been so involved with Angie he would have seen to his father's business affairs sooner and they wouldn't be in this mess now. Hell, what did he know about all these legal matters? Damn little. His father had known he was close to death, Simon was convinced of that, and yet he had done little to get his affairs in order, leaving Simon with the distasteful task.

His mother was little help. She appeared totally ignorant of their financial affairs and was content to have Simon sort through the legal hassles.

A frown drew his thick brows together as Angie filled his mind. Lord, he loved that woman. It seemed a miracle that their love had endured all these years and they were back together. He'd lost her once. Heaven and hell would pass away before he'd let that happen a second time. The pressures on her had been difficult these past several weeks, with her father underfoot night and day, making constant demands. The phone call tonight had come as a surprise, a pleasant one. They'd needed that, both of them.

Somehow, some way, he'd get to Charleston this weekend, even if it was only for a few hours. Angie needed him. Hell, who was he trying to kid? He needed to see her. Not since his early college days had he felt like this. He was supposed to be a serious businessman, yet every spare thought revolved around a wisp of a woman who had claimed his heart so completely that he would never be the same without her. He didn't just want to sleep with her, although that was a part of it. He wanted to care for her, ease her burden with her father and protect her from Clay's angry words. He wanted to laugh with her and hear her laugh in return. And if she needed to cry, then he wanted her to do it in his arms so that he could comfort her as well.

His resolve tightened. He was going to Charleston. Nothing was going to keep him away from Angie. Not ever again.

Glenn was sitting on the sofa waiting for her when Angie returned to the apartment. "Hello."

At her anxious look around, he quirked his head toward the bedroom. "Clay's asleep." He smiled then, his mouth rueful. "I can see why you're so worn down. Clay has a way about him."

"I suppose he talked your ear off," she said with mock seriousness.

"And then some." He paused and chuckled. "There's coffee on if you'd like a cup."

Angie moved into the kitchen and automatically poured two mugs, carrying both into the living room and handing Glenn one. "I don't even know how to thank you for tonight." She felt better than she had in days.

"By having dinner with me tomorrow."

Angie hesitated before sinking into the thick sofa cushion. Seeing Glenn again would serve no useful purpose. He was kind and good, but she wouldn't take advantage of that.

"As friends," he inserted quickly. "I realize that you're involved with Simon now, but I've missed your friendship. There's nothing that says we can't be friends, is there?"

"Nothing," she agreed. If anything she needed a friend now more than at any other time in her life. Only she didn't want to hurt Glenn, and a prolonged relationship, even a friendly one, could do exactly that. "As long as we understand each other." She paused to wipe a weary hand over her tired eyes. "I have a feeling I'm going to end up feeling guilty about this. I don't want to use you as an escape from my troubles."

Glenn ran his index finger along the rim of the coffee cup several times, seemingly unconscious of the action. "I told you this once, but perhaps now it bears repeating. Loving someone means accepting them as they are. I know you love Simon. I'm not saying that doesn't hurt and that I regret the fact you can't love me in the same way. I should have known from the minute you returned from Groves Point that I'd already lost you. Blindly I chose to believe otherwise."

"Glenn . . . stop, please. I'm already beginning to feel guilty."

"No, let me finish. I want you to be happy, Angie. I wish I could say all the bitterness is out of me, but I can't. That will come with time. Us having dinner is as much for me as you. Say you'll come as a gesture toward the friendship we once shared."

Angie studied him for a long time before speaking. "All right," she agreed reluctantly.

"As friends," Glenn reiterated.

"As friends," she echoed softly.

The following morning Clay was much more himself. When Angie woke she found her father dominating the lone bathroom, humming softly to himself as he shaved. The round mirror above the sink was fogged up with steam from his recent shower.

"Better wipe that mirror off or you'll cut yourself," she quipped.

"I been shavin' a lot more years that you been livin'. I know what I'm doing."

Angie laughed, and tightened the cinch of her housecoat. "Yes, Daddy dearest." She was halfway into the kitchen before she realized that this was the first morning in weeks that they'd had a teasing, loving conversation. Usually Clay lingered in bed, claiming that he was in terrible pain and accusing Angie of being no better than those uncaring nurses who didn't give a hoot if he lived or died as long as his medical bill was paid.

She dressed in a simple two-piece skirt and blouse outfit of pale pink colors and returned to the kitchen to cook Clay breakfast.

"You're looking might pretty today," Clay commented. "Are you doing anything special tonight?" The intonation of his voice told her instantly that Glenn had discussed with Clay the fact that he was going to ask her to dinner.

"I might."

"Might?"

"Glenn offered to take me to dinner tonight." She decided to play Clay's game and busily cracked two eggs against the side of a dish.

"Always did like that young man. A smart girl would know what she was turning down. All my days I thought I was raising me a smart girl, but . . ." Abruptly he stopped. "You goin' to dinner with Glenn or not?"

"How could I possibly leave you? A loving daughter would never leave her father alone when he's been so sick and near death."

"Bah, I can take care of myself." He dismissed her concern and sliced the air with a heavy hand for emphasis.

Holding back a laugh was nearly impossible. "You've been telling me for weeks that you've got one foot in the grave."

Clay looked flustered, his impatience growing. "I feel better today."

Angie studied him skeptically. His doctor's appointment wasn't until Monday, and at that not a minute too soon. Until Clay moved in, Angie hadn't realized how much she treasured her privacy. This togetherness was slowly driving her crazy.

"I'm glad to hear that you're more chipper today. Why don't you take a nice walk this morning before it gets too hot and muggy?"

"I might," Clay answered noncommittally.

"And I *might* go to dinner with Glenn."

Clay's fiery gaze clashed with hers. "Then I'll go on that damn walk."

"Which means I'll probably be late tonight."

"Good." Clay's boyish smile went from ear to ear.

• • •

As it turned out, dinner with Glenn was the most relaxing night she'd spent in weeks, maybe even months. He could have taken her to an elegant restaurant and impressed her with wine and song. Instead he chose a Mexican place that was close to her apartment, where the food was fabulous and the atmosphere didn't cost a dime.

"I'll have you know that my agreeing to this dinner has gotten Dad out of the house for the first time since he left the hospital."

One side of Glenn's mouth lifted with a dry smile. "I thought it might. Your father's quite a character."

"I can imagine the things he told you about me last night."

"He's frightened, Angie. Frightened of losing you to Simon. Once you're married, you'll move to Groves Point and he'll be left in Charleston alone. Losing you is his greatest fear. I don't think he can bear the thought of being separated."

"He can move back to Groves Point with me."

"I know that," Glenn replied calmly.

Warming to the subject, Angie clenched her fists. "Dad's got some twisted emotions that need to be sorted through," she declared hotly. Clay's attitude on the subject of the Canfields was relentless. They never openly discussed Simon anymore. Yet the subject loomed between them like a concrete wall they each stepped around and couldn't ignore. "Dad seems to think everyone in Groves Point knows what went on between Simon's family and us. I'm confident that simply isn't so."

"I'm sure you're right."

"Honestly, Glenn," she returned angrily, "quit being such a yes-man. It isn't like you and I don't like it."

Glenn burst into laughter as he placed his napkin beside his plate, his eyes avoiding hers.

Recognizing that he was simply letting her blow off a little steam, Angie felt sheepish. "I'm sorry. I didn't mean that."

"Don't worry about it."

"Quit being so nice," she snapped playfully.

Shaking his head dramatically, Glenn rolled his dark eyes at the revolving ceiling fan. "It's little wonder Clay complains. There's no satisfying you, is there?"

It felt so good to laugh again that Angie's heart swelled with appreciation for this man who was more friend than she had ever known or deserved. She wasn't completely sure of Glenn's motives. In that respect he worried her. No one was that wonderful. There had to be something that he expected in return for this. Quickly, Angie discarded the thought, disliking the cynical meanderings her mind had taken lately and concentrated on having a good time for the rest of the evening.

The following day she sent Glenn a basket of fruit and a brief note as a thank-you for their evening together.

Glenn stopped by the apartment Thursday after work and took Clay out for a walk. Clay didn't look pleased when Angie declined the invitation to join them. Instead she took a leisurely bath, painted her nails and phoned Simon. The evening was young and she wasn't surprised that she didn't catch him at home.

When he phoned her at the shop at their regular time the next morning, she mentioned her call.

"Believe me, I could have used a sweet voice to clear away the insanity," Simon murmured. "Has Clay moved out? You seem to have some free time in the evenings of late."

"Monday," she whispered, purposely avoiding his question. "His appointment with the doctor is the twenty-fifth."

"Believe me, love, the minute he's given a clean bill of health I'm coming to get you. We're going to get married as fast as I can make the arrangements."

"My head is swimming just thinking about it."

"Honey, listen, I'm not making any concrete promises, but I'm doing everything I can to clear Saturday."

Angie felt ridiculously close to tears. Even a few hours in his arms would be enough to wipe out several days of bickering with Clay. "I'll ask Glenn to keep Clay occupied so we can spend more than an hour or so together."

A heavy, stone silence stretched over the line. "Glenn?"

How stupid she'd been to mention him. She didn't want to hide the fact she was seeing him, but she would rather not have discussed it with Simon over the telephone. "Yes, he's the one who's responsible for—"

"You've been seeing Glenn?"

The ice in his voice sent chills up Angie's spine. "Not the way you're implying."

"Then just what the hell is going on?"

Slowly, Angie mentally counted to ten before answering. "He's been helping me with Clay."

"I'll just bet."

Angie's temples began to throb and she pressed two fingers to them to ease the pounding ache. "A customer just came in . . . I've got to go."

"Angie," Simon breathed impatiently. "I didn't mean anything. I think we're both going a little crazy."

"You might be able to come Saturday?"

"I'm coming." He didn't leave any room for speculation. He was going to be there and her heart throbbed with eager anticipation.

"You'll phone me when you get into town, then? I'll be in the shop until noon."

Simon hesitated. "I'll phone."

If Angie felt guilty about going out to dinner

with Glenn it was nothing to what she felt when she asked him if he'd mind keeping her father occupied while she met Simon Saturday afternoon.

Simon hadn't contacted her by the time she left the shop Saturday, which meant he'd probably catch her at the apartment. Normally this would have been a cause for concern, but Glenn and Clay were going for a long drive and would be leaving shortly after Angie arrived back to the apartment.

Their mood was light and teasing when she sauntered in a little after one o'clock.

"Beautiful day, Angie girl. Are you going to join us this time?" Clay asked her on a cheerful note. "Can't see you wasting away in a stuffy apartment when two handsome men are eager for your company."

She was pleased to note the color in Clay's cheeks. "Another time, Dad." She shared a conspiratorial smile with Glenn.

"We'll catch her another day," Glenn interjected.

"But I thought she'd want to come along today." Clay pursed his lips like a discontented child who had been outwitted by his parents.

"I'll join you another day," Angie promised.

"But what are you going to do that's so all-fired important that you can't come with us?" Clay insisted.

Angie looked imploringly to Glenn, but was saved from answering by the doorbell.

Clay stood closest, and swung open the door. Angie couldn't see who it was since Clay was blocking her view. But her father's body language gave her all the clues she needed.

"Hello, Angie." Simon stepped around her father and gave her a phony smile. His gaze went from Clay to Glenn. "I hope I'm not intruding on anything important," he said sarcastically.

≈ Thirteen ≈

Simon recognized immediately that by arriving unannounced to the apartment he'd done the wrong thing. The hurt and confused look in Angie's eyes sliced into his heart. His gaze clashed with Glenn's as he avoided looking toward Angie. Earlier, he'd tried to catch her at the flower shop and had apparently just missed her, according to her employee. The least Angie could have done was wait for his phone call. He was dying for the sight of her. For weeks he'd dreamed of taking her in his arms and loving her until they were both sated and exhausted. Every minute apart these past weeks had been torture. Yet, Angie had gone back to the apartment without even waiting to talk to him and that rankled.

"Simon," Angie said, her dark eyes round and imploring. "What are you doing here? I thought . . ."

"Sneaking behind my back," Clay's pale face turned to his daughter with a hurt look that went far deeper than words. "You two were going to sneak behind my back."

Glenn took the old man's hand and lowered him into the cushioned chair. "Maybe this is the time for the three of you to sit down and talk things out."

Angie's bewildered gaze went from her father's pale face to the intent look marking Simon's features. She stood defenseless between the two of them, knowing that she was about to be forced into taking sides. To one she was a puppet, pulled by the strings of guilt and duty. To the other, impatient in his way, she was a love long-lost.

Clay crossed his arms over his chest and looked straight ahead with stony eyes. Anger and bitterness emanated from every pore. "There's nothing left to say."

"Dad, stop acting like a two-year-old," Angie said looking desperately to Simon. "Why did you come here now, like this? Couldn't you have waited until Clay was well?"

"I believe I'll leave this to the three of you to settle," Glenn murmured, heading toward the front door. "Good luck."

Simon watched the other man's departure with a sinking feeling. Glenn did indeed love Angie. Far beyond what Simon had suspected. He would like to hate the man but discovered that he couldn't. Instead, a grudging respect came, and he wondered if he could have been half as decent over this situation as Glenn. With that realization came another. Glenn wasn't coming around Clay and Angie for his health. Obviously, the man thought there was still a chance he could win Angie. Glenn wasn't a masochist, nor stupid. He was standing ready to pick up the pieces. And now in his impatience, Simon had fallen directly into the other man's hands.

"Simon, maybe it would be best if we sat down. We should be able to reach some kind of understanding." Angie's words helped clear the fog in his mind.

"All right." He moved into the room and took a seat on the sofa. For the first time he studied Angie and was mildly shocked to see how tired and run-down she looked. The faint purple smudges under her eyes were artfully camouflaged with makeup. Her mouth drooped just enough for him to recognize that she was struggling with her composure. By forcing the issue today, he'd done nothing but increase the pressure on her. Silently, he cursed himself.

"I owe you an apology for showing up like this," Simon directed his words to the stiff, motionless man who sat across from him.

Again Angie turned questioning, hurt eyes to him, and Simon damned himself anew. "Then, why did you?"

"I want to marry you, Angie. I'm tired of sneaking around and meeting in hotel rooms. We're consenting adults. There shouldn't be any reason in this world to keep us apart any longer, and if that means forcing Clay to accept certain truths, so be it."

Clay gasped and his eyes narrowed into thin, accusing slits as they centered on his daughter.

"So you've been giving yourself to him. Again."

Angie dropped her face to her hands and again Simon realized that every time he opened his mouth, he was only making things worse for Angie.

"Is this the way I raised you, daughter?" Clay asked in a choked voice that was barely above a whisper. "Your mama, God rest her soul, was a lady. I tried my damnedest to raise you to be just like her. Until now, I didn't realize how miserably I've failed."

"It isn't like that." Angie moved from the sofa and took her father's hands in her own. "I don't know why Simon is doing this, but—"

"I'm doing this because we shouldn't need to hide our love. From the time we were kids we belonged together. As long as I breathe, nothing's going to stand in the way of our happiness."

"Simon . . ." Angie ground out his name. "Don't say anything more. You're only making things worse." Could he be so blind not to see what he was doing to her? She was Clay's daughter, and although he was playing on his recent illness to keep her apart from Simon, that wasn't any reason to drive a wedge between her and her only relative.

Frustrated, Simon rolled to his feet and buried his hands in his pockets. "Listen, maybe it wasn't such a great idea to show up like this. Maybe I should have been patient and played it cool. But for how much longer?"

"Only a few days. A week at the most," Angie cried, not bothering to disguise her hurt.

"Just who are you trying to kid?" Simon asked, watching her closely. He hated to see her on her knees, groveling at her father's feet. "Do you honestly believe that Clay's going to let us find any happiness together? I can guarantee that there'll always be another reason to prevent our marriage."

"You don't know that."

"Angie, look at him. He's never going to give his approval."

Angie shook her head as if to clear her thoughts. "Yes, he will," she cried. "In time."

"I'm through waiting," Simon said on a cold, sober note. "I'm tired of waiting. I want us to get married now."

"It'll only be a little while," she pleaded.

Simon released a low moan of frustration. Angie was living in a dream world. "The doctor will gave Clay a clean bill of health soon, and immediately after that something else will magically appear to delay our marriage."

"That's pure conjecture."

"That's fact," he shouted in return. "We're nearly thirty years old. I'm through with living my life to satisfy parents. I want us to be married and I want it now. Are you with me or not?"

Angie hesitated, slid her eyes closed and inhaled deeply. Here it was. She'd known from the minute

Simon stepped in the doorway that it was coming. With everything that they'd shared, she would have thought he'd know not to do this. The impatient frustrated man standing over her wasn't the Simon she loved. This was a man driven to the limits of his patience, irrational and demanding.

"You can't ask me to do this. Not now."

Simon paused. "When?"

"I . . . I don't know."

In a blinding flash he knew that he was right. Angie was tied to her father and the bonds were far stronger than he'd realized. In pitting himself against the old man, Simon would lose the very thing he treasured most in life. He had to reach Clay.

Simon took a seat across from Angie's father and swallowed down his pride. "Can we lay aside the hurts of the past? I love Angie and I'll spend every second of my life proving just how much. We want your blessing. We need it. Can you overlook everything that's happened and give us your love?"

A full minute passed before Clay spoke. "No words could ever undo the embarrassment and pain your family caused mine."

Simon realized that he should have known the old man would demand blood. "What is it you want then?" He fought back the building anger, clenching his hands so tight that his fingers ached with the effort.

Clay didn't respond.

"What do you want from me?" Simon repeated. Silence.

"More money, is that it?"

"Simon," Angie cried. "Don't do this."

"If you don't want money, maybe I could—"

"All I want from you is to leave my Angie alone. You hear me, boy, leave my daughter alone."

Simon expelled a ragged breath. "That's the one thing I won't do."

"Dad." Angie's voice was so weak that Simon could barely hear her. "Simon and I need to talk."

Clay grunted and crossed his arms. "I suppose you're going to do your talking in that hotel room."

Knowing it was useless, Simon stood and took Angie's cold, limp hand in his. "Let's get out of here. We don't have to listen to that kind of garbage."

Angie stared up at him undecided, her look rotating from Simon to her father. "I . . . don't think I should leave Dad like this. Not now."

"Yes, you can," he argued fiercely, shouting.

Angie pulled her fingers free of his grasp and shook her head, placing her hands over her ears to blot out any protest. "No."

"All right," Simon murmured. He had brought this on himself, by coming to the apartment forcing her into this dichotomy. He was pressuring her to choose between a lifetime of love and loyalty to her father and the reclaimed love she and Simon shared. She couldn't choose one and not betray the other. The crazy part was that all he had ever wanted to do was love Angie and cherish her, protect her, give her his children and love them with the same intensity that he loved their mother. Instead he had set her up for more anguish. Very gently he placed his hands on her shoulders, cupping them. He leaned forward and kissed her lightly on her cheek, shocked at the chilled feel of her skin.

"You know where I'll be," he whispered. It could have been his imagination, but Simon thought he felt her stiffen as if to pull away. His heart plummeted to the very depths of hell. He was so close to losing her, and powerless to reach out to her now. Angie Robinson was the only woman he ever truly loved, and he had somehow managed to louse up their relation-ship . . . a second time.

"I'll talk to you later," she whispered in return.

For two hours Angie wrestled with her emotions. The more she thought about what Simon had done by coming to the apartment the angrier she became. Maybe he was right. Maybe Clay would always find an excuse to keep them apart. But now wasn't the time to catapult her into making a decision. For days she had eagerly anticipated being with Simon, looking upon his visit as a time for renewal and rejuvenation, mentally and physically. Their time together was to be a brief oasis in a life whose route had taken her deep into the arid, lifeless desert. In the past weeks, they'd both been taxed to the limit of their endurance with family pressures. They'd needed this time for their sanity.

Clay sat so motionless that for an instant Angie wondered if he'd stopped breathing. When Simon had gone she'd half expected her father to blast her with a fiery tirade of insults. In the past he'd done exactly that, knowing how much it hurt her. Instead his eyes revealed a deep, bitter pain that words wouldn't easily erase. So they didn't speak, but sat like strangers, yearning to reach out to each other and not knowing how.

When she could endure the agony no longer, Angie stood and reached for her purse.

"I . . . need to think," she whispered. "I don't know when I'll be back."

"You're going to him," Clay said with cruel certainty.

Angie's jaw sagged, prepared to argue. Dejected, she closed her mouth. She'd hadn't given thought to where she was going, only that she couldn't tolerate another minute in the tension-filled apartment.

"Don't lie to me, girl. You're going to him."

Clay was right, that's exactly where she was going. "I'll be back" was all she said.

The ride across town took her through heavy traffic, giving her plenty of time to think. She loved Simon, had loved him nearly all her life. When she'd taken the money and left Groves Point twelve years ago, something keen and vital had died within her. For a long time she couldn't look at men without experiencing a deep, harrowing pain. After a while, more Clay's sake than her own, she'd started dating again. If he was tall, Angie decided she preferred someone shorter. If he was quiet and introspective, she found him boring. If he was intelligent and opinionated, she wished for someone dull. After a while, Angie gave up dating completely. Until Glenn . . .

The front desk at the Hilton gave her Simon's room number and she marched across the lobby, her indignation building. She loved him, but she couldn't allow him to pressure her this way.

She'd hardly had time to knock when the door was opened. "Thank God you came," he whispered.

"Why?" The word barely made it through the tightness in her throat. "Why did you come to the apartment? Didn't you stop to think what would happen?"

"Angie, listen—"

"No," she cried, "you listen. I want to marry

you. All I'm asking for is a little patience. My dad is damn lucky to be alive. I'm not prepared to do *anything* to endanger his health and that includes upsetting him the way you did this afternoon. You . . . you may have blown everything. I can't understand you."

Simon pushed the hair off his brow and splayed his fingers through his thick hair. "I think I went a little crazy when I learned Glenn was coming around."

She couldn't believe that he could possibly be jealous of Glenn. "He's been wonderful." She said this to imply that Simon hadn't been.

A grimness tightened his face. "Of course he has. Glenn loves you. Why else do you think he's been hanging around."

Angie struggled with the building discontent. "Glenn came to apologize for that last scene . . . He saw the toll that nursing Dad was having on me and offered to give me a break."

Simon heard this with a frown of distaste. "You don't really believe that, do you?"

Angie raised angry, stricken eyes to him. "Of course I believe that. It's exactly what happened."

Simon's snort was filled with disgust as he stalked to the far side of the room. "Are you so naive as to believe that your father didn't have a hand in that? I don't doubt for a minute that Clay was responsible for Glenn's sudden appearance."

Angie stared at him in shocked disbelief. She

thought she knew Simon so well but discovered that she didn't know him at all. Together they owed a great unpayable debt to Glenn Lambert. Glenn's love and patience had given her the courage to face the past and go back to Groves Point. Even after she'd returned to Charleston, he had loved her enough to step aside until she'd sorted through her feelings for Simon. Angie didn't try to kid herself. None of this had been easy for Glenn, but he had acted with a patience, love and understanding that was, at times, almost superhuman.

A frozen, deadly silence iced the room.

"You may be right." Angie's words shattered the cold quiet. "But we both should thank God for Glenn."

Simon lifted one dark brow at her, assimilating her words. "I didn't realize your feelings were so intense."

"Stop trying to make something sordid out of Glenn's affection for Clay and me. He at least had the common decency not to pressure me into—"

"Choosing between your father and me."

"Yes," she finished, her voice quavering.

"That's the beauty of the situation," Simon returned with heavy sarcasm. "With Glenn there would be no decision to make. Clay would love to see you married to him."

"I've already agreed to be your wife. What else do you want?" Swallowing down a sob, Angie sank onto the side of the queen-size mattress, struggling against the rising hysteria. She had so looked forward to this weekend with Simon. She couldn't believe that they would waste this valuable time together fighting.

"Where's the ring I gave you, Angie?" His slicing gaze fell to her bare fingers.

One hand curled over the top of the other. "With Clay feeling the way he did I couldn't wear it. Surely you can understand that."

"No." Simon's voice was deadly calm. "I'm afraid I can't."

"All right, I should have worn it," she cried, knowing he was hurt and hating herself for being so weak. The ring, the most precious piece of jewelry she owned, was locked in a desk drawer at Clay Pots. A hundred times she'd thought to slip it on her finger and decided against it, knowing the sight of it would cause an argument. She'd been so tired lately and hadn't wanted to battle Clay at every turn.

"What's in a ring? Right?"

Her head snapped up, positive she hadn't heard him correctly.

His eyes narrowed on the soft rise and fall of her breast.

"Simon," she whispered pleadingly. "Your ring is a symbol of your love. I'm sorry I haven't worn it."

"Not sorry enough." He sat beside her

impatiently and tugged at the buttons of her blouse, jerking it open and off her shoulders so quickly she hadn't time to protest.

Shocked and appalled, Angie was stunned.

"If you love me so much," he taunted, "I'll let you prove it."

"Simon." She struggled briefly, shocked at the remote look on his hard face but was stopped by his roaming hands.

He caught her by the shoulders and whirled her around so that he could release the zipper of her skirt. Hurried fingers gripped the waistband and pushed the material over her hips and onto the floor.

"Simon, what are you doing?" she cried, attempting to cover herself.

In answer he stripped off his shirt and slacks, his eyes avoiding hers.

"I love you," she murmured in a choked voice, "only don't do this to me. This isn't making love."

He was a stranger whom she didn't recognize.

Tears swam in her eyes as she slumped onto the mattress. "Simon, what's come over you?"

He joined her on the bed, lowering her so that her head rested on the thick pillow. "You keep saying that you love me so much." He leaned toward her, and his free hand boldly caressed her breast, cupping it. "I want you to show me how much." He continued to fondle her breast, teasing the nipple with this thumb by rubbing it over and over until it rose hard against the lacy material of her bra.

Angie was numb with disbelief. This couldn't be happening to her. Not with Simon. He'd always been such a gentle, kind lover. He had given of himself, never taken. Their lovemaking was special, a sharing of their intense joy of each other.

"Why are you doing this?" she begged, her hand stopping his.

"Why?" he echoed cruelly. "Because you don't love me enough," he said and positioned himself so that he was leaning over her. Harshly, he took her mouth, grinding his lips over hers until Angie pushed herself free.

"You think I should have been more diplomatic with your father."

"Yes," she cried. "He's ill."

"The time for diplomacy is past. Either you want to be my wife or you don't."

"Oh, Simon," she whispered, needing his tenderness. "I do love you." She turned her face to him and hesitantly laid her fingers over his rigid jaw. He was angry and hurt and lashing out at her in a way she'd never expected.

Momentarily, his steely eyes softened. "Then marry me. Today. Now." Again, his mouth claimed hers, parting her lips with a deep, languorous kiss. Angie locked her arms around his neck and kissed him hungrily in return. He burned a hot trail of kisses down the scented hollow of her throat to just above her braline. Impatiently he stripped away the bra and teased the pink tips of her breasts with circling, flickering caresses of his tongue until Angie gasped at the startling pleasure and arched her back, burying her fingers in his hair. She was helpless to the hot, searing need he was building within her. Nuzzling her neck with his mouth, his hands continued their arousing movements until Angie was writhing beneath him. "Simon," she whispered, "please."

"Do want me?" he taunted in a low voice.

"Yes," she pleaded.

"Enough to come away with me today for the rest of our lives?"

Angie's eyes flew open and she went limp against the mattress. Simon raised his head, his eyes boring into hers. "Today," he repeated starkly.

"I . . . can't. Don't ask that of me."

"I just did."

"All I want is your love." She raised her head and tried to kiss him, but he held himself stiff and unyielding avoiding her touch.

"I won't settle for what's left over when Clay takes advantage of you," he said harshly.

"But I'm offering you everything," she said desperately. "Everything. If you'll only be patient. I love you so much." The last was offered on a soft sob that erupted from her parched throat.

A long moment of tormenting silence passed as his expression clouded over with bitterness. "Words no longer satisfy me," he ground out. "Only actions." His mouth came down in a kiss that was devoid of tenderness. Angie's hands were flattened against his bare chest, intent on pushing him off her and freeing herself. At the slightest pressure, Simon's arms surrounded her, pressing her into the soft bed. Slowly, subtly his kiss changed from punishing to pleasuring. His tongue invaded her mouth, searching for the secrets of the moist recess.

With a moan, her hands lost their purpose and slid over his powerful shoulders, drawing him to her. Simon didn't seem to know what he wanted: to torture her or to show her his love. In the end it was a lot of both. He took her with a savage urgency that left her trembling and shaking in his arms.

His body remained pressed to hers when he lifted his head; his face was twisted with an unreadable anguish, his eyes squeezed tightly closed. An eternity passed before he spoke. "Dear God, did I hurt you?" he asked, his voice low and raw with emotion.

She tore herself from his grasp when he tried to reach for her and bring her into the comfort of his arms. Grabbing her clothes, Angie dressed as quickly as her trembling hands and body would allow. Her fear was that if she didn't escape fast enough Simon would hurt her again. She couldn't have tolerated him touching her. Simon hadn't made love to her. He'd been looking for a way to hurt her and succeeded beyond reason.

She prayed that he wouldn't try to stop her. Her throat was burning with the effort to suppress the sobs. She hesitated as she turned toward the door. Simon was sitting at the end of the bed. His face was buried in his hands; his shoulders hunched over, giving a profile of abject misery. As she stepped into the room, Simon raised his head, his eyes pale and haunted.

"Angie, wait."

She didn't hesitate, but briskly stepped across the room.

"Please."

Her hand tightened around the doorknob and she paused. "Clay always said you were a spoiled rich boy," she whispered through her pain. "I never believed him until today."

Dejected and utterly defeated, Simon didn't try to stop her as she pulled open the door and walked out of his life.

In the long days that followed, Angie had plenty of time to think over their last meeting. In many ways she understood why Simon had behaved the way he had. That didn't excuse his actions, but granted her the time to be more forgiving. In the beginning she decided that when he phoned

286

she'd treat him aloofly, with mild contempt. A miserable week passed and she realized she would have given her soul to hear from him. Another week and she recognized that Simon never planned to contact her. He'd given her the option either to marry him then or it was over. She had made that choice.

Not knowing what had transpired, Clay watched her guardedly for several days. The second afternoon following the doctor's appointment, he moved back to his own place and showed up only at periodic intervals. They never mentioned Simon.

Glenn called once a week to chat and ask how she was doing. Their conversations were brief and one-sided. He didn't ask her out, intuitively recognizing, she supposed, that she'd turn him down. In many ways Angie would always be grateful to Glenn. He had been a good friend when she needed one most, but she had abused that friendship and was paying dearly for it now. She didn't know if Clay had asked Glenn to visit her or if he'd come of his own initiative. It didn't seem to matter and she didn't inquire.

When she realized that she wouldn't be hearing from Simon, Angie prayed fervently that she would become pregnant, and wept acid tears the morning she learned she wasn't. For a time she thought he might contact her if only to ask if that last time together had given life to his seed. Angie didn't know if her tears were from bitter disappointment that she wasn't going to have his child or that Simon didn't seem to care enough to find out.

Slowly, each day a test, Angie began to gain her perspective again. She had a good life, a meaningful one. Her business was profitable, and she made casual inquiries into opening a second shop on Calhoun Street near Marion Square. At the end of the third week, Angie discovered that she could smile again and occasionally even laugh.

The hottest days of summer came in late August and the muggy afternoon heat was unbearable. Angie took long walks along the beaches, watching the children play in the sand. The world seemed full of children and young mothers. In a month she would be thirty. Simon would be thirty. Their birthdays were only a few days apart.

Friday afternoon, a half hour before closing time, Angie was working in the back of the shop when she heard the small bell ring, indicating that someone had entered. She set aside the centerpiece she was constructing from dried wildflowers and approached the counter. Her eyes met the elegant ones of Georgia Canfield and she faltered slightly. Quickly regaining her composure, Angie braced her hands on the counter.

"Hello, Mrs. Canfield."

"Hello, Angela."

She looked calm, but out of place in something as common as a flower shop. "It's a lovely place you have here."

"Thank you."

"I understand you named it after your father."

"Yes." Angie didn't feel all that comfortable with this woman. She couldn't understand what Simon's mother would be doing here unless something had happened to Simon. An instant of panic filled her mind, but she dismissed it quickly. Knowing Georgia Canfield, she was sure the woman would tell her soon enough the reason for her unexpected visit.

"I never wrote to thank you for the wreath you sent for Simon's funeral."

"I understand that you were very busy."

"Yes." She hesitated. "My husband's death was quite a shock."

"I'm sure it must have been."

The phone rang and Angie excused herself to take an FTD order from Boston. As she wrote it out, she noticed that Georgia sauntered around the shop as if she hadn't a care in the world. The woman was amazing.

Replacing the receiver, Angie cleared her throat softly. "Was there something I could do for you, Mrs. Canfield? I'm sure this isn't a social call." Angie wanted to fill this order before closing time and there were only a few minutes left. She didn't know what kind of game the woman was playing, but she wasn't in the mood to go along.

Georgia Canfield sighed appreciatively. "Charleston is such a lovely city."

"Yes," Angie agreed, letting her eyes drop to the FTD order. "Mrs. Canfield," she said, breathing heavily, "I don't mean to be rude, but if you have something to say, I wish you'd say it. I don't have time to play cat and mouse with you."

The older woman paled slightly. "If you insist on being direct then I shall. I'd like to know what happened between you and my son?"

Angie's smile was bittersweet. "You'll have to ask Simon that."

"My dear girl, I would hardly come three hundred miles to quiz you if I wasn't forced into doing so." Her voice was calm and even. The only outward sign that she was angry was the drumming pulse in her neck.

In spite of herself, Angie smiled anew. "No, I don't suppose you would."

"My son is deeply in love with you."

Angie walked briskly past the woman to the flower case. Opening the refrigerated cabinet, she withdrew several long-stemmed roses and a variety of other flowers she would need for the arrangement.

"Doesn't that mean anything to you?" she demanded.

"Yes," Angie admitted with an uncomfortable feeling of guilt. "It means a great deal."

"Do you love him?"

"I don't believe that's any of your business."

A small, admiring smile twitched at the corner of the older woman's mouth. "I strongly suspect that you do."

Angie's fingers tightened around the unstripped stems in her hands. The thorns cut unmercifully into her hands. "If you'll excuse me."

"No," the woman barked.

Angie turned surprised at the uncharacteristic rise in the older woman's voice. "Twelve years ago, I paid you ten thousand dollars to leave Groves Point," she said in a low, controlled voice. "Today I would offer you everything I own if you'd agree to come back."

≈ Fourteen ≈

"I promised myself I wouldn't intrude on Simon's life a second time," Georgia Canfield continued, more subdued now. "But my son needs you." Her gloved hands were folded primly in front of her creaseless linen suit. "I thought at first it was my husband's death that had affected him so greatly. But now I believe it's you."

"Mrs. Canfield, if Simon loves me as much as you say then he would have come back for me."

"And if you love him as much as you say," she fired back, "you'd make the effort to go to him. Listen, Angela, you're not the woman I would have chosen for Simon, but I've already had my chance at handpicking one wife. All I want is my son's happiness, and if that means you then I'm willing to accept you as a daughter-in-law."

"Maybe we should understand each other, Mrs. Canfield," Angie shot directly back. "I don't play bridge and have no intention of learning. I don't want to have anything to do with the country club and I plan to be far too busy to join all the charities that interest you. Furthermore, if I come back to Groves Point I plan to bring my flower shop with me and work in it until the babies come."

The frown that drew the delicately lined

eyebrows into one stiff curve relaxed at the mention of children. "You do want children?"

"A house full."

"And you wouldn't restrict me from seeing them?"

"Mrs. Canfield, we've all made mistakes. I don't hate you. I couldn't. You're Simon's mother, and the very things I love about Simon are the best parts of you. You would be the only grandmother our children would have. They would need your love just as much as Simon and I would."

The older woman's tight mouth relaxed and trembled at the corners. "My dear," she whispered so softly that Angie had to strain to hear, "perhaps you would consider being a guest speaker at the Garden Club someday."

Angie's own voice was soft and quivering. "I'd enjoy that very much."

Mrs. Canfield opened the clasp of her purse, took out a dainty lace handkerchief and dabbed the corners of her eyes. "Believe me, I didn't expect to resort to tears, but I've been terribly distressed about Simon."

"What's happened?" A niggling fear invaded her happiness.

"I think it would be best if you saw for yourself. Do come soon, Angela."

"I'll be there within a week."

"Thank you."

"No, Mrs. Canfield," Angie whispered through the emotion blocking her throat. "Thank you."

Saturday morning, after furiously making arrangements with Donna regarding the flower shop, Angie packed her bags. Her first stop on the way out of town was at Clay's. Apprehensive, she sat in her car an extra minute to compose her thoughts. This was the moment she dreaded. She was going home to Simon, to where she'd always belonged, but in doing so she was pulling away from the loving, protective arms of her father. Long ago Angie had recognized that Clay's actions had been motivated by love. Fear and pride had played a large part in his actions, too, but mostly there was love. He had used his health as a means of emotional blackmail so that she stood torn between the two men she loved the most in the world. Clay thought he'd won.

He opened the door and gave her a look of mild surprise.

"Angie." He glanced at his wristwatch. "It's barely eight. What are you doing up so early?"

She gave him a kiss on the cheek and raised her eyes to his. "I'm leaving, Dad."

The smile drained out of Clay's face inch by inch, leaving him pale and deadly sober. "You're going to him."

Angie nodded. "It's where I belong."

He smiled a little sadly and hunched his shoulders forward as he slumped onto the sofa. "I guess I've always known you would."

"Thank you for not trying to stop me."

"I wouldn't," he said, and his low voice was edged with pain. "You go to him, Angie girl, and tell him for me that he's the luckiest man in South Carolina."

Sitting beside her father, Angie took him by the shoulders and gently laid her soft cheek to his jaw. "I'll be moving Clay Pots with me."

Clay nodded and closed his eyes. "You've done well for yourself. I've been proud of you from the minute your mama laid you in my arms for the first time. No matter what I've said to you, I've always been proud you are my daughter."

"Dad . . . do you remember how Groves Point gave us a second chance after mom died? It'll do that again. I want you to move back . . ."

"That's impossible, Angie." He lowered his head and studied his clasped hands for a heart-wrenching minute. "I've never told you how deeply I regret taking that Canfield money."

Angie laid her hand over his. "I was the one who took it."

"No," he argued. "Not only did I convince you to accept that money, but I took the chance of giving you the college education you deserved. I wasted all those thousands on a pipe dream."

"Dad—"

"No, I want you to listen. I've got some money saved, not much, a few thousand. When you go to Simon I want you to give him that with the promise that I'll repay him the rest of the ten thousand when I can. I realize it's a little old-fashioned, but I want you to think of this as your dowry."

"Oh, Dad," she whispered hoarsely, fighting back tears. "I should have told you."

"Told me?"

"Remember when I sold Petal Pushers?" She gave him a moment to absorb the meaning of what she was saying.

He looked puzzled, a deep frown narrowing his brow into three thick lines as he studied her.

"That was our business, yours and mine. You worked as many hours as me. Often more. I sold it, invested the profit and returned the ten thousand dollars to the Canfields with twelve years of compound interest."

Clay's puzzled frown turned to one of amazed stupefaction.

"We don't owe the Canfields a penny."

"Why didn't you tell me?"

She shrugged one shoulder. "I wish now I had."

Clay hugged her close, squeezing her head with his long arms. "Go to him, Angie. With my blessing and with my love."

"Thank you, Dad," she whispered through a heart pounding with happiness.

The drive took the better part of seven hours. Angie stopped twice. Once for gas and another time to grab a sandwich and something cool to drink. As her car ate up the miles, Angie grew more content. She felt as if she was going home, really going home after a long time away.

She didn't stop in town, but drove directly to Twenty Acres and Simon's house. Their house, her mind corrected, with its four spacious bedrooms, office and family room.

Prince barked when she pulled into the long gravel driveway, but stopped when she climbed out of the car and gave him her hand to smell. The short-haired black dog seemed to recognize her and wagged his tail in greeting. Laughing, she found a stick, threw it into the woods and watched him scramble after it.

The back door was jerked open, and Angie turned to see an angry scowl on Simon's face disappear into one of shocked disbelief.

"Angie," he whispered as if seeing an illusion. He rubbed his hand over his eyes. "Is it really you?"

Unexpectedly, she felt shy. It took everything within her just to meet his gaze. "Hello. The real estate man said I might want to look at this place as a possible home for a family."

Slowly he came down the concrete steps,

measuring her words as though he couldn't believe that she had come back to him a second time. Every instinct in him urged him to pull her into his arms and thank Almighty God for giving him another chance with this woman. A crippling thought paralyzed him on the bottom step. No woman would return to him after the way he'd abused her body and spirit. Not unless there was a damn good reason. Angie had every right to hate him.

Dear Lord, could she be pregnant? She just said she was looking for a family home. After all the weeks that he had prayed she would conceive his child, the thought that she had given life to his seed when he had treated her savagely seared a hole through his heart. He remembered the way she'd put her arms around him and tried to kiss him back, but he wouldn't allow her that. The look on her face when he'd finished abusing her body had haunted him these long weeks, filling him with self-loathing that was so intense he could barely look in the mirror. She'd been so shocked, so appalled. And yet she tried to give of herself, tried to love him. Only he wouldn't let her. His intent had been to take, not give. Even when she attempted to join their bodies' natural rhythm, he'd intentionally made it discordant. Now she was pregnant with his child and Simon didn't know if he should thank God or curse Him.

A gnawing fear froze the smile on Angie's face as she watched Simon. The happiness that had filled her heart left as quickly as it came. He didn't want her. "Simon," she whispered achingly, "please say something."

"Why did you come?" He wanted to hear her say the words, telling him what he already knew. From the way she spoke, he'd know her feelings on the matter. He studied her face, praying he'd find some clue that she didn't hate him though she had every right.

"Why?" she repeated, dropping her gaze, her mind discounting his mother's visit. So this was to be Georgia Canfield's ultimate revenge. She'd persuaded Angie to return to Groves Point when Simon no longer loved or wanted her. "If you need to ask, then you don't know." She felt sick with defeat and failure. Her stomach heaved and she placed a calming hand on her abdomen.

He stiffened, his body tensing into a rigid line as her hand moved to her stomach. He closed his eyes and groaned inwardly. The hurt, betrayed look told him everything. His eyes flickered open. No matter what her feelings were, Simon realized, he wanted that child enough to fight her in every court in the land for the right to raise him. It didn't matter that his son had been conceived in anger and pain. The child was a part of Angie he had never dreamed he'd have. His gaze narrowed menacingly, and frightened, Angie took a step in retreat.

"I shouldn't have come," she whispered miserably.

Her fear sobered him and he drew back slightly. She would be a wonderful mother, gentle and caring. Tender and nurturing. No man in his right mind would tear a child from her arms. She'd die before she would let it happen. If she wouldn't have him, then, by god, he'd give the child his name. Some way, somehow he'd make her marry him.

"I'll make the arrangements for the wedding as soon as possible."

She swallowed and stared at him. "Don't you think we should discuss things first?"

"No," he barked, taking her by the elbow and escorting her into the house. He pulled out a kitchen chair and sat her down. Pacing the area in front of her, he threaded his fingers through his hair angrily. "Maybe I should get you to the doctor first. Who have you seen?"

"Seen?" Good heavens, Simon wasn't making any sense whatsoever. "The only person I've talked to was your mother."

"My mother," he raged furiously. "You went to her and didn't have the common decency to tell me? I wondered, God knows I wondered, but I thought you'd contact me first. I never dreamed you'd go to her."

"I didn't go to your mother," she shouted back on the verge of tears, her voice shaking. "She came to me."

"How did she know?"

Angie blinked twice. "She must have guessed . . . Simon . . ." She paused, drew in a deep breath and shook her head. "What are we talking about?"

"The baby," he told her evenly. He knelt beside her and took her hands in his. Shocked eyes met tender ones and Simon smiled at her with a fierce gentleness that robbed her lungs of oxygen. "After everything I've done and said to hurt you, can you find it in your heart to forgive me and marry me?" He drank deeply from her eyes and continued. "I love you more than life itself. These past weeks have been a living hell, knowing what I'd done to you."

He thought she was pregnant! She laid her hand on his smoothly shaved cheek and smiled. When she spoke her voice was filled with tears. "You may not want to marry me when I tell you something."

"I've wanted you from the time we were sixteen. Not once in all those years has that changed."

She dropped her forehead to his and closed her eyes. "Simon," she whispered brokenly. "I'm not pregnant."

The words went through him like a bolt of lightning. "You're not?"

"No. I wanted to be so badly. Every day I prayed that I was." Shyly, she closed her eyes. "If I was pregnant, then I'd have an excuse to come to you."

"Come to me? Oh, my sweet, darling Angie." He couldn't believe that this incredible woman loved him after all he'd put her through. He'd suffered the agonies of the damned these weeks without her, knowing that after what he'd done he couldn't go back to her. Pleading for her forgiveness wasn't enough to take away the pain of their last meeting. "Oh, love, I don't deserve you. You're far too good for me."

Through joy and tears and an immense relief, her arms sneaked around his neck and she smiled at him through the watery haze. "Simon, dear Simon, I love you so much."

His arms came around her, crushing her. His eyes were dark with emotion as his mouth found hers with all the aching longing of this last separation. "I hope to God you're sure," he whispered against her lips, "because I'll never have the strength to let you go again."

"I'm sure. Very sure." She kissed him in all the ways he'd taught her, her tongue seeking and finding his until she was faint with joy and longing.

Simon's mouth and hands moved over her with a fierce tenderness until their breaths became mingled gasps of pleasure. They strained against each other wanting to give more and more.

When Simon stood, lifting her in his arms, Angie tossed back her head until her radiant gaze met his. "Where are you taking me?" she teased, finding his earlobe and sucking it until she felt the shivers race through him.

"Who said you weren't pregnant?" he asked and traced the delicate line of her chin with his forefinger. "After today I can guarantee you that will change."

And it did.

Center Point Large Print
600 Brooks Road / PO Box 1
Thorndike ME 04986-0001 USA

(207) 568-3717

US & Canada:
1 800 929-9108
www.centerpointlargeprint.com